It was all Aki could do to stay on her feet, she felt so ill.

She staggered a few more steps and was about to fall when Gray grabbed her and held her up. Even though his face was covered by his mask, she could sense his sympathy . . . and fear.

As the Phantoms swooped closer, Jane shouted, "They're right on us, sir! Closing in fast!"

"Jane, take the lead!" ordered the captain. He lifted Aki's limp body and began to run with her. All she could see were glowing Phantoms—writhing, teeming, leaping over the ruins. They were right on the heels of the Deep Eyes.

"Fire in the hole!" shouted Jane.

Suddenly, a tremendous explosion shook the ground, and the air rippled with bio-etheric energy. *It's almost like my dream!* That was the last thing Aki remembered before she passed out in the captain's arms.

FINAL FANTASY™
THE SPIRITS WITHIN

A Novel by John Vornholt
Based upon Final Fantasy: The Spirits Within
Screenplay by Alan Reinert and Jeff Vintar
Based on an original story by Hironobu Sakaguchi

A
MINSTREL®
BOOK

Published by POCKET BOOKS
New York   London   Toronto   Sydney   Singapore

This book is a work of fiction. Names, characters, places and incidents are products of the author's imagination or are used fictitiously. Any resemblance to actual events or locales or persons, living or dead, is entirely coincidental.

A MINSTREL PAPERBACK *Original*

A Minstrel Book published by
POCKET BOOKS, a division of Simon & Schuster, Inc.
1230 Avenue of the Americas, New York, NY 10020

ISBN: 0-7434-2351-8

First Minstrel Books printing July 2001

10 9 8 7 6 5 4 3 2 1

A MINSTREL BOOK and colophon are registered trademarks of Simon & Schuster, Inc.

Printed in the U.S.A.

For Katherine, Mistress of the Web
—*J.V.*

FINAL FANTASY™

THE SPIRITS WITHIN

CHAPTER I

The young woman gazed in amazement at the bizarre, alien landscape stretching before her. It was red, parched, and barren. Weathered rocks and burned branches were twisted into strange shapes, as if blasted by unknown forces. The ground was scarred with deep, black crevices, and it looked as if it hadn't rained in centuries.

Lifeless dust floated on the hot breeze, and the sky was filled with golden clouds. Sunlight filtered through the clouds, giving them a fierce glow that was oddly beautiful. In the distance, the curve of a giant moon peeked over the horizon. Like everything else, the moon was beautiful, frightening, and unreal. It was so close, the young woman felt as if she could touch it.

Aki Ross shifted uneasily on her feet, because

1

she didn't know where she was. The wind rustled her shoulder-length brown hair, tossing it back from her face. She whirled in every direction, but there was nothing moving except the ageless dust. She knew she had to be patient and wait—for whatever was coming to this blasted wilderness.

It began as a low rumbling sound—far away but coming closer. The young woman fought the impulse to run, and she held her breath as the rumbling grew louder. The roaring noise washed over her like a wave, and the ground began to shake. Rocks tumbled down, and Aki was tossed off her feet . . .

And into her laboratory chair! That was where the scientist found herself when she awoke. When Aki realized it had all been a dream, she let out her breath and rubbed her eyes. Her fingers reached for the holographic control panel floating before her, and she easily worked the shimmering device.

When she was done, the display read, "DREAM FILE SAVED. 12/13/2065."

Aki pressed a blinking light, and the hologram disappeared. Scanners pulled back from her body and retracted into the chair, and the magnetic connectors clicked off. Free at last, Aki floated weightlessly out of her chair, slowly drifting upward. Now she used her legs to give a real push, and she zoomed across her laboratory on the scientific shuttlecraft, *Black Boa.* She had to enjoy the low gravity while it lasted, because it would end when they left orbit.

Near a viewport, she grabbed a handhold and came to a gentle stop. Wistfully, the young woman gazed down at the serene blue Earth, so far below the shuttlecraft. She only wished the planet could be as peaceful as it looked from up here. Once the *Black Boa* had been a science ship with a full crew. Now it was just her, circumnavigating the globe, looking for life forms.

The dream is always the same, she thought. *I'm standing, waiting for something. It's over the horizon—coming for me. And then it's over. If they knew about these dreams, they'd shut me down. But I need to know what the dreams mean.*

I think the answer may lie with them *down there. The question is, will I be in time to save the Earth?*

* * *

Flames engulfing its hull, the sleek, black shuttlecraft reentered Earth's atmosphere. Minutes later, the *Black Boa* was streaking over North America, descending upon the island of Manhattan—now part of the world that had been abandoned.

The small ship landed between two crumbling buildings, shooting dust and debris everywhere. Burned-out cars, piles of concrete, and seas of trash surrounded the dark shuttlecraft. Search-lights from the ship probed the broken husks of abandoned buildings, looking for anything still alive.

Aki stood nervously on the landing platform, dreading this part of the operation the most. She wasn't scared of facing death—that part was normal. No, she was scared of failure, of not finishing their experiment. Time was running out for all of them, especially her.

For once, it would be nice to get in and out quickly, thought Aki. *But it was never easy, not down here.*

The hatch opened beneath her feet, and the landing platform slowly lowered Aki to the street. She adjusted the combination scanner/flashlight she was wearing over her left eye, then she touched the energy gun hanging on her right hip. Its flare-like disperal pattern was the only way to see the enemy.

All of her instruments searched for life, but it was so much easier to find death.

The cold wind carried no scent of life, and Aki shivered. She activated the scanner over her left eye, and it beeped in response. The lenses began to focus, sending holographic images to her mind.

Once the center of a vibrant city, Times Square was now a dark, brooding wasteland. Decrepit buildings loomed over the remnants of the dead civilization. The *Black Boa*'s searchlights explored the husk of an old building, and the light cast a shadow of her slim figure. Aki tried to look calm and businesslike, despite the fear gripping her stomach. After all, this was her job—finding the spirits left alive.

To the naked eye, it appeared as if she was the only living thing for miles around. But eyesight didn't catch everything. Aki stepped away from the *Black Boa,* trying to peer through the dust they had stirred up. There was nothing to see but the broken windows and dark ruins that had once been stores and theaters. Old New York had turned into the world's biggest haunted house.

She had to work quickly. It wasn't a question of *if* they would find her, but *when.* So Aki drew her pistol, checked the setting, and aimed skyward. She fired, and a bright flare arched across Times Square, bathing the area in an eerie glow. Sparks of light floated to the ground like radioactive snowflakes.

She checked her eye scanner and frowned, because there was still no sign of life. "Where are you?" she muttered.

Aki lowered her gun and turned on her wrist scanner, which had greater range. The device glimmered like a neon armband, and a small beacon beeped and blinked on the underside of the bracelet. The display read, "NO LIFE FORMS."

The young scientist pointed her arm in one direction, then another, waiting for the scanner to tell her which way to go. When the beeps sounded stronger to the north, Aki leveled her flare gun and started off at a brisk walk. She double-checked the compass on her left arm, because she sure didn't want to get lost down here.

As she walked through the shadowy ruins, Aki's heart pounded in time with her crunching footsteps. She could sense that she was being watched, and she knew she should turn back. But there might not be another chance to retrieve the sixth spirit—not in this unlikely place.

Aki widened her light beam, but it didn't do much to dispel the darkness. Every doorway or busted window could be a hiding place for *them*. The young woman searched a clump of twisted metal, but it didn't reveal anything. Behind her, the searchlights of the *Black Boa* looked far away.

Aki lifted her gun and fired another flare over the gloomy square. As the sparks floated downward, she could see faint outlines, like animals caught in a flash of lightning. Only these were *not* animals— they were lumpy, translucent creatures with enormous heads and whipping tentacles. They looked like balloon animals made of neon gas, but they weren't harmless, like balloon animals.

Phantoms!

As the sparks from her flare began to fade, Aki knew she had to complete her mission, or die trying. She whirled around and saw more Phantoms hovering between her and the *Black Boa*. She was cut off. They were everywhere, lurking in every corner and doorway. Aki gulped and shook off the terror. She still had a few seconds to find the spirit that survived in this devastated city.

Now Aki ran through the towering ruins, darting between twisted hulks and piles of rubble. The scanner signal was strong and getting stronger. That meant she was getting closer to her target with every footstep!

Trying to follow her readouts, she dashed down a narrow street. Instantly she knew she had made a mistake coming this way, and she whirled around to escape. But a huge Phantom popped out of an alley, blocking her path. With whipping tentacles

CHAPTER 2

As the writhing, shimmering Phantoms drew closer, Aki heard a rumbling noise above her head. She gazed upward through a hole in the roof to see a black troop transport. Dark figures clad in gray armor and robotic headgear dropped through the dusty night air. On their way down, they released containers that exploded all around her. The gas spread along the ground and hardened into a shimmering gel.

Deep Eyes, thought Aki with relief and anger. She always figured that if the Phantoms didn't get her, the Deep Eyes would; but she didn't think *both* of them would catch her. *I'm a magnet for trouble today.*

One by one, the soldiers landed throughout the area, with the gel cushioning their fall. As the Deep Eyes rose to their feet and formed ranks, the substance on the ground evaporated. Their eye scanners blazed as they aimed their weapons and opened fire on the Phantoms. Aki had to drop to a crouch and scurry out of the line of fire.

She stared in fascination as their energy beams ripped into the Phantoms, making them clearly visible for an instant. As the monsters swelled with electrical discharge, they grew brighter and brighter until they suffered structural breakdown. One by one, the Phantoms vaporized into glistening red clouds.

The leader of the Deep Eyes whirled and pointed at her. "This is a restricted area! Do not move!"

"What's she doing here, Captain?" muttered another soldier, his voice sounding youthful.

"I don't know, but we're getting her out." The captain motioned to his men to pull back, just as Aki saw an apparition fly over his shoulder.

"Behind you!" she shouted.

Half a dozen Deep Eyes turned on the Phantom and blasted it to pieces. While they were distracted, Aki bolted toward a crumbling building.

"Halt!" bellowed the captain. "I said *halt!*"

Aki paused to catch her breath and survey her scanner. She could hear the Deep Eyes' angry voices behind her, shouting at one another in confusion.

"Let's move, people!"

"Two coming through the east wall!"

"Sarge, hold your fire. Those tanks are flammable!"

Suddenly, the whir of blades grew louder, and a searchlight from the sky landed on Aki. "There she is!" shouted a voice. Aki checked the direction on her scanner and ducked deeper into the building.

An explosion ripped the air, and Aki felt a blast of heat on her back. *Those idiots blew up one of the oil barrels with their careless firing,* she decided. Maybe it would slow them down long enough for her to find the sixth spirit.

"Ryan! Neil! Jane! Let's go!" shouted a voice. She heard footsteps pounding the pavement just outside the building, and she kept moving. The Deep Eyes were right on her tail, and they wouldn't let her get away again.

Arm extended, following the beacon, Aki charged into the devastated building. The beeping sounded louder than ever, and she knew she was getting close. Only a few more feet . . .

From the darkness, a hand gripped her arm and whirled her around. Aki stared at the helmet-like eyescope of the captain of the Deep Eyes. "Just what do you think you're doing?" he demanded in a voice that was muffled by his eyescope.

She pointed desperately at her wrist scanner. "There's a life form in here!"

"There hasn't been life here in years," scoffed the leader.

"Well, there is now!" Aki tried to break away from his forceful grip, but he held her tightly.

"Life form or not, I'm taking you in," vowed the captain.

"Fine, take me, I don't care. But not until I extract this life form!" With a deft move, Aki twisted out of his grasp and strode away.

She passed the sergeant, who only muttered, "It's gonna be one of those days."

Crouching, dashing from post to post, the soldiers followed Aki deeper into the building. She could hear their footsteps skittering behind her, but she focused all her attention on her wrist scanner. As she heard the Deep Eyes talking to one another, she began to figure out their names. The one who did the most talking was Ryan, the sergeant, followed by Neil and the female, Jane.

The blinking beacon led Aki to an old, cracked fountain. Above them, the ceiling was gone, and moonlight streamed into the eerie building. Aki looked around the base of the fountain, and her eyes lit up when she saw her goal.

"Captain," said the soldier named Jane, "the transport is not going to wait for us much longer."

"I understand that," answered the leader. Aki

could feel him hovering behind her. She tried to ignore the soldiers as she bent down to inspect her fragile prize. Growing through a crack in the floor was a tiny, bedraggled weed. The scanner flatlined and stopped beeping.

"It's in bad shape," Aki said worriedly.

"Oh please . . . tell me we're not risking our necks for this plant!" grumbled Ryan.

"I wouldn't even call it a plant," answered Jane. "It's a weed."

"I wouldn't even call it a weed," scoffed Neil.

Aki pulled out a small spade and began digging. "I need a minute to extract it."

The Deep Eyes looked around nervously, and Ryan said, "Miss . . . that's a minute we don't have."

"Phantoms! We have incoming!" shouted Neil.

Aki looked up from her work to see Phantoms oozing through the walls all around them. She hurried her digging and was able to free the fragile plant from the ground as the soldiers dropped into firing position.

"Uh, Captain, we need to get moving," warned Ryan.

"Understood, Sergeant."

"We've got a lot of Phantoms here!" shouted Jane worriedly.

Aki carefully placed her precious plant in a container just as gunfire lit up the old building. She snapped the container shut while gleaming energy beams streaked over her head.

Ryan shouted, "We need to get outta here! Could you hurry please, miss?"

"Done," answered Aki, rising to her feet. All around her, the Deep Eyes were firing wildly at the advancing shapes and tentacles.

"Captain?" said Neil. "Just so you know, I agree with the 'let's get outta here' thing."

"Duly noted," answered the captain, firing away. They were backed up against the fountain, when suddenly a huge Phantom rose from the cracked marble and whipped a long tentacle at them. The captain promptly blasted the creature until it exploded in a red haze, and the fountain crumbled to dust around them.

Aki felt a hand reach for her holster. "Can I have this, please?" asked Jane, taking her flare gun. "Thank you."

The soldier jammed the flare onto her rifle and fired it at the floor of the old building. Flaming sparks bounced off the floor and streaked toward the ceiling. As the shards of light floated down, they could see dozens of creeping, amorphous Phantoms surrounding them.

"I hate to say 'I told you so,' " muttered Ryan.

"We're surrounded!" said Aki with a gasp.

"No lie!" snapped Jane, pumping beam after beam at the deadly foe. All of them were looking for a way out, but there didn't seem to be one.

"All right, everybody," said the captain calmly. "Just relax."

Without warning, a bright light blasted them from above, and Aki looked up at the huge hole in the ceiling. The troop transport was up there somewhere, trying to help them.

"Captain, we gotta get to higher ground!" said Jane, retreating from the Phantoms.

The captain looked around and spotted a staircase against the rear wall. He motioned them toward the stairs, shouting, "Go! Go! Go!"

In the lead, Aki dashed up the stairs, but she found the way blocked by a pile of rubble. She had to scramble over the pile, but she kept moving. Now *she* was in a hurry—to get her specimen back to the laboratory to continue her experiment. The Deep Eyes were right behind her, all except for one. Bravely, the captain stayed at the base of the stairs, raking the Phantoms with gunfire. He was trying to cover their escape.

"Up here!" shouted Neil, trying to get his attention. The rest of them were safely on the next floor—the captain was the only one still in danger.

Surrounded by Phantoms, the leader jumped onto the stairs and scrambled over the pile of rubble. A Phantom swooped toward him, and he rolled onto his back and blasted it. The luminescent creature exploded, but the staircase cracked beneath the captain. He dropped down to ground level, and his rifle skittered out of his hands.

"Captain, come on!" shouted Jane.

Ryan motioned wildly. "You can make it! Keep moving, Captain. Phantoms are right behind you!"

With fluorescent shapes swirling all around him, the captain made a mad dash up the rubble-strewn staircase. Jane reached down and held out her hand, and she caught him when he slipped in the debris. With a mighty tug, she pulled him to safety while his comrades blasted the Phantoms behind him.

Aki didn't know why she should care, but she breathed a grateful sigh of relief.

"You okay?" asked Jane.

"Yeah," breathed the captain.

"All right, everybody!" shouted Neil. "Here they come."

The Deep Eyes fired again as another wave of Phantoms rose from below. But there were too many of the monsters, and they had to retreat again. Just as the Deep Eyes were surrounded, black cables came dropping through the hole in the ceiling. The soldiers quickly grabbed the cables and hooked them to their armor. With whooshing sounds, they were drawn up into the sky.

Aki felt a strong arm grab her around the waist, and she looked up to see the captain, holding her. He gave a tug on his line, and the two of them lifted into the night sky just as deadly tentacles whipped at their feet.

CHAPTER 3

As soon as the Deep Eyes and their passenger were safely inside the transport, the ship fired thrusters. Blowing dust and debris everywhere, the ship roared away from the haunted streets of Old New York.

Aki clutched the box containing the precious plant as she sat among the Deep Eyes. One by one, they began to remove their metallic eyescopes. She was surprised to see how young and vulnerable Ryan, Neil, and Jane looked. They were hardly any older than she. The only one who didn't take off his eyescope was the captain, who seemed to be lost in thought.

"You okay?" asked Ryan, gazing at the scientist.

Aki gave him a faint smile and nodded.

Suddenly, the captain growled, "Can you give me one good reason why I shouldn't arrest you?"

Aki stiffened and narrowed her green eyes at the hulking leader. She wished he would remove his eyescope. "I am Doctor Aki Ross. I have clearance to be here."

"Not unlimited clearance," he answered. "And not without authorization."

Aki scowled. "Listen, Captain, I don't have time for this."

The soldier leaned toward her. "Do you realize you've just risked the lives of my squad and me?"

Using her wrist scanner, the scientist checked the readings on the fragile plant and breathed a sigh of relief. It was still alive. "Look," she said, "I don't want to talk about it. The fact of the matter is, it was *worth* the lives of you and your men."

"You and your *men?*" scoffed Jane.

Ryan laughed. "She thinks you're a man!"

"I think she's an idiot," muttered Jane.

Neil winked at her. "I know you're not a man."

"I think *you're* an idiot, too," snapped the female soldier.

"Well, I *do* want to talk about it," insisted the captain, staring at Aki. "Did it ever occur to you that maybe we would have *volunteered* to risk our lives had we been given a choice?"

"Well, nobody asked you to save me," answered Aki.

"I don't believe this," grumbled the captain. "You have not changed a bit."

Aki watched him as he slowly removed his eyescope. She gasped when she saw his square jaw, short hair, and piercing eyes. "Gray?"

The captain placed his eyescope on his lap and stared at her. "Yeah. Nice to see you, too."

Captain Gray Edwards, thought Aki, feeling strange emotions swirling in the pit of her stomach. He was a part of her life that she had tried to forget. Of course, since he was in the Deep Eyes, she was bound to run into him someday. Now she did feel guilty about risking his life . . . and the lives of his squad. But she hadn't invited them—they came on their own.

* * *

The troop transport soared over the dark ruins of Old New York, headed toward a glittering Barrier city in the distance. A massive, irregular tent of protective energy fields shielded the part of New York where humans still lived. It was one of forty-two still functioning barrier cities. The rest of Earth belonged to the Phantoms.

The transport soared around the shield and descended toward the city that looked almost normal.

With the roar of thrusters, the transport dropped low and touched down on a runway in a deserted airport.

Clutching her container, Aki followed the Deep Eyes off the transport into a large air lock. Or maybe it was a hospital—there were a lot of medical devices, examination tables, scanning machines, and monitors. As they entered, they were separated from the technicians by a thick pane of glass. It was obvious that someone thought they might be infested.

"Welcome back," said a technician. He tried to muster a smile, but he looked serious about his duties.

Aki turned and found Gray looking at her. He quickly turned away. "We're clean," Gray told the man behind the glass.

"Let's make sure of that, shall we?" answered the technician.

The Deep Eyes began to grumble. "I hate gettin' scanned," said Neil.

"These scanners are probably worse for us than the Phantoms," muttered Ryan.

The captain's voice boomed over the complaints. "People, let's just do this thing, all right?"

"Yes, sir!" answered his squad in unison. It was clear to Aki that they would do anything Gray ordered them to do.

Ryan, the sergeant, stepped first onto the scanner platform. Aki could see his image on a nearby monitor, but it wasn't his physical image—it was his spirit. It looked blue, shimmering, like a heat wave made of ice.

"Okay. Next," said the technician.

Ryan stepped off, looking bored, as if this were an everyday chore. Jane followed him onto the platform. As the glimmering image of her spirit appeared on the monitor, Neil remarked, "Looks like you've gained some weight."

"It's called upper body strength, Neil," the female soldier shot back. "Get a girlfriend."

A moment later, the technician motioned Jane off the platform and looked at Neil. Aki turned to Gray and whispered, "You know, my security rating allows me to bypass this."

He frowned. "Not today it doesn't."

Neil passed the scan with a clean spirit, while Aki twisted her hands nervously. If she told them *why* she couldn't go through the scan, they would throw her into a cell. When Gray took a step closer to the machine, Aki took a step closer to him. "Listen, Captain, I think we—"

Gray scowled and stepped onto the platform. "I don't care what you think, Doctor. You're getting scanned just like everybody else."

Suddenly an alarm sounded, and everybody whirled to look at the monitor . . . then at the captain. Gray's spirit was not all green—there were blinking red spots of infestation!

A cylinder dropped from the ceiling, trapping the captain like an animal in a cage. For the first time that day, Gray looked scared, and so did his squad. They were all talking at once, saying it must be a mistake. But Aki knew it wasn't a mistake. She had seen those images before.

"You came in contact with a Phantom, sir," said the technician, looking grim. "Please remain calm. Administering treatment shield."

Gray pushed his hands against the inside of the cylinder, looking as if he wanted to break out. Aki quickly stepped up to the glass and peered at the technician's data. "What level is he?" she asked.

"It'll be code red in three-and-a-half minutes," the man answered.

Aki surveyed the room and spotted an operating table at the back. "We have to treat him now," she said.

The technician shook his head. "I'm sorry, but that's impossible. We'll transfer him to the Treatment Center."

"There's no time for that." Aki rushed to the wall and pulled a lever. The protective cylinder rose to the ceiling, and Gray stepped out, looking dazed. Aki pointed to the operating table, and the Deep Eyes rushed to help Gray. By the time they got him to the table, Aki was already working the controls, getting ready for the operation.

After Gray laid down on the table, she picked up a hypo and made sure it was loaded with enough anesthesia to knock him out. The gruff captain looked worriedly at her. "Aki, there's something I need to say—"

"Don't try to speak." She put the hypo to his neck and gave him the injection. A second later, he closed his eyes and was asleep. The scientist activated the table, and it came alive with a dozen blinking holographic controls. The Deep Eyes crowded around the table, but they still gave her enough room to work. The soldiers acted tough, but now they looked like frightened children.

A holograph of Gray's body floated above his real body. It showed his normal blue spirit, but there were also bright red tentacles writhing within his body. The infestation was getting worse by the second, and soon it would drive out his own spirit. Once that was gone, so was he. There wasn't time to think—only to work.

Aki pushed a button to magnify the infested area. "How much more time?"

"Less than three minutes," answered the technician. "When he reaches code red, the treatment shield won't be able to hold the alien particles."

Without wasting another second, Aki activated the laser scalpel. The beam drilled into Gray's body, and Aki guided it with the holographic controls. She watched his floating image as the red tentacles were burned away by the laser beam. It was a painstaking process, because she had to get it all. If she left even one millimeter of Phantom particle, he would die.

From the corner of her eye, Aki could see the clock counting down. She was working as fast as she could. When she was down to one last tentacle, she grabbed the controls with both hands, working to get it all.

At last, I'm done. Or am I? The display insisted that she had missed a section of the infestation. An urgent beeping sounded in her ears.

"What's going on?" demanded Ryan.

"Where did it go?" asked Jane nervously.

Desperately, Aki brought up another holographic view of Gray's body. The captain's eyes rolled back in his head, and he went into convulsions. As his body flopped around on the table, the technician shouted, "We've lost contact! Infestation is moving deeper."

"I'm tracking it," said Aki.

"There's no time," insisted the technician. "You're gonna lose him."

In the holographic image, Gray's spirit twisted in agony. People were shouting at her, but Aki ignored them all and kept working.

"His treatment shield is failing!" warned the technician.

Aki peered intently at Gray's anguished spirit. She finally spotted it—a faint trace of red. She bore down with the laser scalpel just as the buzzer sounded, and the clock hit zero.

Ryan groaned, Neil swore, and Jane bit her lip nervously. Aki still didn't know if she had gotten the particle in time. She leaned over Gray's still body, willing him to be alive. Suddenly, he opened his eyes and peered at her. His spirit image turned as clear and blue as a mountain stream, and Aki smiled as she pushed the button to turn off the equipment.

With cheers, the Deep Eyes gathered around their leader and helped him to sit up. Although he was alive, Gray couldn't stop shaking. Aki wanted to comfort the captain, too, but she kept her distance. Her life was already complicated enough.

"Don't worry," Aki assured him. "You'll be back

to normal in no time." She picked up her plant container and marched toward the exit.

"Wait a minute," said the technician. "We need to scan *you* for infestation."

Aki stopped, wondering if she should simply refuse. Either way, she would be arrested. The one thing she had to do was protect the sixth spirit in the palm of her hands.

Suddenly, a familiar voice cut through the silence in the room. "That won't be necessary. I'll take responsibility."

Aki whirled around to see Sid, her boss and mentor. The gray-haired scientist smiled at her, and she held up the plant to show him she had been successful. Both of them knew what was at stake, but they were the only ones. With his security clearance, he could overrule any lab technician.

"Hey, Doc!" called Ryan. "Thanks for saving him."

Aki nodded as Sid quickly escorted her out of the room. She wanted to look back at Gray, but she knew she had better not. With any luck, she would never see the handsome captain again.

* * *

Jane gazed suspiciously at the departing scientists, then glanced at her comrades. The captain was resting peacefully. "What's with her?" she asked.

"What's with her and the captain?" wondered Ryan.

Neil scoffed. "What's with her and that stupid plant?"

CHAPTER 4

When the small, crumpled plant was placed into a spectral analysis chamber, Aki finally breathed a sigh of relief. The laboratory assistant stepped back and looked expectantly at Sid and Aki. The old scientist waved and motioned to his console. "Forward me the Phantom data and everything regarding the five spirits collected so far."

"Yes, Doctor," answered the aide.

Although Aki had been here many times, it was always inspiring to come to the Bio-Etheric Center. Her hopes, her dreams, her reason to live were all tied up in this place. In fact, the fate of the human race was in the hands of Sid and his assistants. The young woman stepped behind the great scientist and gazed over his shoulder at his holographic readouts.

"Spirits?" she whispered. "I thought we weren't supposed to use the 'S' word."

Sid chuckled. "Don't get smart with me. Now let's see if that plant does the trick."

On his shimmering screen, there were images of the five energy fields collected so far—the first five spirits. As Sid worked his controls, the energy waves merged into a colorful pattern. Everyone in the room held their breath as the spiritual energy from the plant was added to this kaleidoscope.

To Aki's delight, the new addition blended perfectly with the others, forming a serene band of colors. This bright wave was the exact opposite of the Phantoms' eerie appearance. Aki could almost feel the healing powers of these ageless spirits.

The spectrum was not complete—spirit types were still missing—but Aki was still bursting with excitement. "It's a match! We've found it," she blurted.

"Yes, the sixth spirit," answered Sid in a reverential voice. He glanced her way and added, "Your little scene today broke nearly every protocol."

Aki said nothing as she turned from the glittering array of instruments. She went to the machine where the fragile plant was resting, and she gently picked it up. She touched its stems and leaves as a mother would touch a baby's fingers. "How long do you think this would have survived outside the Barrier?"

"You know there are elements in the Council and military just waiting for an excuse to shut us down," Sid continued.

That brought a scowl to Aki's face. "Look, twenty years ago, who discovered this energy in the Phantoms? *You.* And who proved the same energy source existed in humans and every life form? *You!*"

Sid shrugged modestly, but Aki went on. "You made it possible to harness that energy for ovopacs, scanners, even the Barrier. The Council knows that—they trust you. Doctor, we're so close to proving it—"

"We still need this part and this one here," answered the scientist, pointing to his holograph. "Two more pieces, and we've solved the puzzle."

"Exactly!" said the young woman.

"And we need to be *free* to find those pieces." Sid reached into the bottom shelf of his work station. "I want to show you something, Aki."

He handed her a small book bound in linen. Aki had never seen it before. It didn't look large enough to be a reference book or a textbook. She found a bookmark, which turned out to be a dried leaf, and she opened to that page. There was delicate handwriting. "What is this?" she asked.

"Read," suggested the old man.

So Aki read aloud, " 'All life is born of Gaia, and each life has a spirit. Each new spirit is housed in a physical body.' " She stopped and looked up with curiosity. "Doctor?"

"Go on."

" 'Through their experiences on Earth,' " she read, " 'each spirit matures and grows. When the physical body dies, the mature spirit, enriched by its life on earth, returns to Gaia, bringing with it the experiences, enabling Gaia to live and grow.' "

Sid gave her a slight smile. "It's my old diary. I wrote that forty-three years ago when I was the age you are now." He took the book from her and ignited it with a lab burner.

"Sid!" exclaimed Aki, horrified at his act. Within seconds, the book was nothing but cinders.

"Remember what happened to Galileo," said her old friend. "They threw him in jail because he said the Earth was not the center of the universe. That could happen to us. Our ideas are unpopular, Aki. If you have any notes or records that could be used against you, destroy them. Keep them up here." He pointed to his head.

"Right," agreed Aki, feeling disheartened. Just when they faced their greatest discovery, they also faced their greatest danger. After years of fighting and retreating from the Phantoms, humans had lost all patience. They just wanted to live—it was survival of the fittest.

When she turned and walked away from him, he added, "And stay away from your friend, the captain."

Aki stopped and gave him a look, as if to say *excuse me, is that your business?*

Sid went on, "He saves your life—you save his life. This leads to that. . . . I was young once, too, you know."

"Doctor, there is a war going on," said Aki, turning toward the door. With a sigh, she added, "No one's young anymore."

* * *

That night, Aki was plunged back into the strange, alien landscape she visited in her dreams. Twisted rocks and gnarled stumps rose over the blasted desert, and the sun beat down through the thick clouds. The wilderness was dead, drained of all life, yet it held a strange fascination. The young woman stood on the shifting sand . . . listening, waiting.

Soon she heard the eerie rumbling sound, getting louder. The ground under her feet began to shudder, and she weaved back and forth. On the jagged horizon, there was suddenly movement—swarming, like giant insects. Before she had a chance to run, Aki realized it was Phantoms! An army of Phantoms was headed straight toward her . . . roaring with rage. And they were solid beings.

The young woman whirled to escape, but she was faced with the same awful sight in the other direction. A second army of screaming, misshapen aliens was charging toward her, tentacles writhing. With a start, Aki realized they were warring armies, meeting on this barren plain to destroy each other.

With howls and wails, the Phantom armies clashed on the field of battle. In all the frightful things they had done to humans, they never fought as savagely as this. Aki stared in horror, until she could stand no more. . . .

She bolted upright, only to find herself in her own bed. Her chest was heaving, and her breath came in panicked gasps. Aki tried to calm herself, but that was impossible when she couldn't explain the dream. She was afraid it meant death for all of them.

* * *

General Hein stood before the Emergency Council, which numbered eight grave politicians. With the government scattered, this body made most of the decisions for the war-weary land. *The army keeps the country from falling apart completely,* thought Aki, *and they know it.* That gave the charismatic warrior, General Hein, great power when he addressed the Council in its crowded chambers.

The general pointed to a mammoth holograph of Space Cannon Zeus hovering in orbit over Earth. Then he highlighted the meteor in the Caspian Mountains, from where the invaders first sprang.

"Ladies and gentlemen of the Council," said Hein, "could you please explain *why* Zeus was ready a month ago and we haven't used it? If we attack the meteor with this, we will eliminate the Phantoms at their source."

On cue, a beam shot from the space station and struck the meteor in the desert. In a frightful blaze, the source of the Phantoms was suddenly gone. There was much impressed chattering in the room, and Aki heard grumbling from Sid sitting beside her.

The chairman of the Council rose to speak. "General Hein, calm down," he said impatiently. "At our last meeting, we voted six to two to *postpone* using the Zeus Cannon to attack the Leonid Meteor. We have reconvened today to vote on that very issue again."

He pointed toward Aki and Sid. "Now I'd like to

ask the director of the Bio-Etheric Center to speak. Dr. Sid, please."

The scientist ignored General Hein's glare as he rose to address the Council. Hein finally joined his military cohorts in the gallery. The three-dimensional image generator changed scenes as Sid approached. Now it showed a close-range view of the enormous meteor. Phantoms were being spawned at an amazing rate from a crater in the top of the ugly black rock.

"Thank you," Sid began. "As you all know, the Phantoms' nest is in the Leonid Meteor that landed here thirty-four years ago. What you see now are the records of every assault on the meteor to date."

The audience watched horrifying images of attacks against the meteor. Armed men, bazookas, missiles, tanks, bombs—every type of conventional weapon was used—but nothing stopped the evil spawn of monsters. "Physical attacks have had utterly no effect," concluded the doctor.

The simulation continued, and a nuclear bomb destroyed half the surrounding landscape. The meteor was still there. Worse yet, it continued to disgorge hundreds of gruesome Phantoms. The murmur of voices in the Council chamber fell to a hush.

"This scene took place three months ago during a full-scale bombardment," said the doctor.

The view changed, and ribbons of bio-etheric energy consumed the meteor. Now the Phantoms died by the score, their tentacles whipping in convulsions before they shriveled to dust. General Hein and his aides smiled with satisfaction, although it was Sid who had discovered this deadly technology.

"Now, please note, the Phantoms outside the meteor are indeed destroyed." Sid pointed to various images of death on the display. Moments later, the view shifted to charts and readings taken from their subterranean sensors.

"However," warned Sid, "inside the meteor, many that were dormant came to life. As you see, overall Phantom density remains the same. The newly risen aliens respond to the attack by burrowing even deeper into the Earth."

There was excited discussion in the hall, and one of the Council members leaned forward. "Now this is very interesting to me, Dr. Sid," she remarked. "We see the same thing during surgery when using bio-etheric lasers on Phantom particles, do we not?"

"Yes, indeed we do!" exclaimed Sid. "You see, the injured particles *escape,* burying or digging themselves deeper into a patient's body. And when we increase the laser power to destroy these deeper particles, we have had incidents resulting in further injury to a patient. In some cases, death."

Aki thought of the frantic race to find the last Phantom particle in Captain Gray as she watched these particles burrow deeper into the Earth. Suddenly, a powerful beam came from the orbital station, and it pierced the Earth like a dagger. The inner core of the planet was ripped apart by the assault.

"And what exactly does *that* mean, Doctor?" asked the chairman, pointing to the shimmering images.

"It means there's a very good chance the beam from the Zeus Cannon *will* burn the Phantoms in the meteor," answered Sid.

"Exactly!" crowed General Hein. "Thank you."

Sid shook his head glumly. "Now, however, it also means that the beam energy may be too strong, injuring the Earth."

"Injure the Earth? You mean the Gaia?" asked a second politician.

The old scientist sighed. "I mean—"

"You mean the spirit of the Earth?" asked the Council member, pressing.

Sid thought for a moment, then he nodded bravely. "Yes. The spirit of the Earth."

The room buzzed with amazed conversation, because few people would admit that the Earth was a living being. It had been that way a hundred years ago, and it was still that way. They were at war, and humans seemed more endangered than the planet. The chairman banged his gavel on the block, trying to restore order in the chamber.

Aki waved to Sid and whispered, "What are you doing?"

"I *know* what I'm doing," he answered. "And whatever *you* do, keep your mouth shut!"

General Hein laughed openly. "This is ridiculous! Doctor, with all due respect, did you come here just to talk about some Gaia theory? To tell us that the planet is . . . alive? That it has a . . . spirit? That's a fairy tale, Doctor, and I'm sorry, but we don't have time for that."

"It is not a fairy tale," insisted the scientist. "It is true."

General Hein pretended to point his fingers like a gun. "Oh, so if I point a gun at the Earth and fire, I'm not just making a hole in the ground. I'm killing the planet?"

Some members of the audience laughed, while others begged with them to consider the idea. Aki looked away, feeling sorry for the doctor. Why hadn't he taken his own advice and kept quiet about these beliefs?

The chairperson struggled to maintain order. "Dr. Sid, the Gaia theory has not been proven."

"Even if Gaia does exist," said another, "won't

we still have to remove the Phantoms? I think if there is any chance of success, we should take it. Don't you agree?"

Sid nodded patiently. "Well, uh, of course I do. But there is an alternative to the space cannon."

"Another method?" she asked.

"Yes. A means of disabling the Phantoms."

"Please," said the Council member, pointing to the holographic display.

Sid nodded, looking relieved to get the discussion back onto practical matters. He put up the data that Aki had helped him compile earlier that day.

"As we know," he began, "the aliens display a distinct energy pattern. Now it is a fact that two opposing bio-etheric waves placed one over the other will cancel each other out. It is theoretically possible to construct a wave pattern in direct opposition to the Phantom energy."

Hein sniffed. "The operative word there is 'theoretically.'"

Sid went on, trying to ignore him. "We have been collecting energy signatures from a variety of sources. From animals and plants, we have assembled such a wave and are nearing completion." As he spoke, the Phantom particles on the holographic display disappeared.

"Members of the Council," said Hein with a

smirk on his face, "gathering plants and animals from around the world to fight the Phantoms is utter nonsense. The Zeus Cannon is a proven, effective weapon. It will kill Phantoms. Can we afford to wait for some crazy invention, some army of touchy-feely plants and animals? An invention that offers no solid evidence that it will destroy the aliens?"

At those words, Aki jumped from her chair. "There is evidence!" she declared. Sid waved his hands to stop her, but Aki went on. "Our partially completed energy wave has successfully stopped Phantom particles from spreading through a terminally infected patient."

The entire hall reacted with stunned silence, followed by claims of disbelief. It took a lot of gavel banging to quiet the chamber again, and all eyes were on Aki.

"Doctor," asked the senior member, "do you claim to have evidence that a terminal patient has been cured?"

"Not cured," replied Aki. "The wave is not complete. But we've succeeded in containing the particles safely inside the patient."

"Ah," declared the general, "where is the proof?"

"Here!" Aki opened her tunic and presented them with a startling view. Attached to her chest was a blinking, metallic chest plate. The device created a wave containment field that controlled the particles within her. General Hein and several others looked repulsed by the sight, then she caught sight of Captain Gray Edwards in the back of the room. He was staring at her in amazement.

Aki pushed a switch on the device, and a holographic display shimmered on. Now they were clearly visible—the Phantom particles writhing inside her body. To make sure everyone could see her, she approached the big display in the center of the room. After she patched in her signal, her infestation glowed at ten times normal size. There were gasps from all over the room.

She bravely lifted her chin and tried not to look at Gray's shocked face. Sid took her arm and detached her from the master display. With a few parting words to the Council members, he escorted her out of the buzzing chamber. Behind them, loud arguments broke out.

When they got into the hallway, Sid whispered, "You may have bought us some time, Aki. But I wonder—at what cost?"

"Doctor, I can't keep hiding in the background while you protect me," protested Aki. "I want what life I have left to mean something."

The old man gave her a pained expression. "You

listen to me. When we find the seventh and eighth spirits—"

"*If* we find them. What we need now is some luck."

"Luck has nothing to do with it," snapped Sid. "Faith and hard work, girl. 'Cause there's no way you're going to die before *me!*"

CHAPTER 5

The earthbound city of New York, or what was left of it, was protected by a glistening bio-etheric Barrier. This irregular shield was maintained by equipment erected on the ends of high pillars. They looked like tent poles, holding the shimmering shield above the city. The only way to get to these lofty workplaces was by vertical gondolas.

Sid and his team had turned one such gondola into a research laboratory. From here, they could monitor vast distances on both sides of the Barrier, while staying connected to electricity and communications from below. The gondola would be Aki's home until she could return to the *Black Boa*. The Deep Eyes had retrieved her shuttlecraft, but lots of paperwork was needed to get it out of impound.

City lights glistened just below Aki's roost in the gondola. But on the other side of the shield, where the Phantoms ruled, there was only darkness. It would be a good place to conduct her research, thought the young scientist, except for one thing: She wasn't alone. Captain Edwards hovered in the doorway. She hadn't invited him, but there he was.

"The Council decided to postpone firing the Zeus Cannon," said Gray with a smile.

"I guess I put on a good show," muttered Aki. She concentrated on her instruments, trying to ignore him.

Gray stuck his head in the door. "Mind if I tag along?"

"You'll probably get bored," said Aki with a shrug.

The handsome captain jumped onto the gondola just as the doors slid shut. A moment later, the cabin shook slightly, and they took off from the platform. A holographic display showed the car gliding through the darkness on taut cables as it skimmed the sparkling Barrier.

In this case, the window was more spectacular than the displays, and Aki found herself gazing at the glittering city far beneath them. So many lives . . . in such danger.

"So, what are you doing?" asked Gray, moving close to Aki in the cramped cabin.

She didn't even bother to reply, because she was working and he wasn't. It wasn't her job to be a tour guide.

"Oh, I see, you are giving me the silent treatment," said Gray, moving close to her again.

Aki whirled around to get away; instead she ran right into the hulking soldier. Not moving a muscle, Gray just stood in her way. Reluctantly, she went back to her instruments.

"I'm scanning the city for the seventh spirit," answered the scientist.

He nodded and looked as if he understood. *But how could he?* Aki shot past him and crossed to the scanners on the other side of the cabin. *Maybe if I leave him alone, he will leave me alone,* she thought crossly.

* * *

As the gondola glided high above the city, bio-etheric energy bristled from the supporting pillars. The Barrier glowed a bright orange for an instant as the gondola shot past a transformer.

On the boarding ramp, a laugh sounded. The

sergeant put down the long-range telescope and checked his wrist scanner. He spotted Aki and Gray's sprits right away on the speeding gondola. The car was moving way too fast, and he wanted them to take their time.

Ryan looked up at the maintenance structure above him, where his comrade, Neil, was hard at work on the wiring of the control box.

"Hurry up, Neil!" he called.

"Relax, Sarge," answered the soldier, still messing with the wires. "I've almost got it. Oh, look who's here. . . . Hi, Jane!"

Ryan looked back to see the third member of their trio. Jane went by the book, and she might not appreciate their idea. So they hadn't told her. As the athletic soldier strode across the platform, she gave them a disgusted look. "What do you think you're doing?"

"We're just gonna strand 'em for a while," answered Neil. "Hey, don't look at me, it was *his* idea." He pointed to the sergeant.

"This was *your* idea?" asked Jane.

Ryan shrugged. "We're just helping the captain out a little."

"Yeah, come on, Jane," said Neil, "where's your sense of romance?"

"You've seen how the captain looks at her," said

47

Ryan with a grin. Overhead, sparks flew from the wires where Neil was working.

"It's *amore,* baby!" shouted the happy soldier. The pulley shut off, and the thick metal cable screeched to a halt. Out there in the middle of nowhere, the gondola had also come to a dead stop. *There, that would give the two old friends a little time together.*

* * *

Aki punched the controls of the doctor's gondola, but it didn't do any good. They were frozen tight, and the cabin was swaying in the wind. "What's going on?" she muttered.

"It's probably just a glitch." Gray watched her ply the controls with no results, and he finally said, "Listen, Aki—"

"I'm still mad at you," she broke in.

"*You're* mad at me?"

She nodded. "Leaving your eyescope on? Not telling me who you were? That doesn't seem a *little* childish?"

"Hey, well," stammered Gray, "I was just a little upset when you packed up and left for the Zeus Station without saying a word."

"Well, now you know what was going on, all right?"

The captain scowled. "Yeah, *now* I know."

"My operation had to be done in zero-grav, okay?" said Aki quietly.

"Fine . . . and how about the fact that I was sent there on a job and you wouldn't even see me?" Gray crossed in front of her, demanding an answer.

"I was probably helping Dr. Sid collect spirit waves," she answered.

"Well, now I know."

Aki murmured, "So I'm sorry."

"Well, me too!" snapped Gray. "So . . . we're both sorry." After they both sighed gloomily, Gray asked, "Will you tell me about them?"

"About what?"

"About the spirits you've collected."

While she tried to get the gondola moving again, Aki began her story. "I was infected by a Phantom during an experiment. Normally, no one could have survived."

"How did you?"

"Dr. Sid created a membrane around the infection, keeping me alive. So the first spirit wave was *me.*" Absently she touched the device on her chest. "The second, was a fish."

"A fish?"

Aki kept busy with the controls. "The third was a

deer I found in a wildlife preserve outside Moscow. The fourth was a bird." She laughed slightly. "Ever tried to track a sparrow from outer space? It's no fun . . . what am I saying? You probably would love that."

"You're right, I probably would."

She went on, "And then there was that plant I collected from Times Square."

"I thought that was number six."

"What?" murmured Aki, deep in thought.

"You skipped one."

"The fifth was a little girl, dying in a hospital emergency room. I retrieved the sample in time but she, uh—" Aki's voice grew hoarse. She could barely go on, but she did. "I told her everything had a spirit. Dogs, cats, trees, little girls, even the Earth. I told her that she wasn't dying—just returning to the Earth's spirit, to Gaia."

The young woman sniffed back her emotions. "She told me that she was ready to die. She said I didn't have to make up stories to make her feel better." Aki shook her head sadly. "Only seven years old, and ready to die."

Gray tried to comfort her, putting his arm around her shoulder. "I'm sorry," he whispered.

But her grief and fear were still vivid, and Aki

pushed his hand away. "I have work to do. I have to find the seventh and eighth spirits—"

A moment later, she stopped working, unable to figure out how to get the gondola moving. It was like so much in her life—hung up, suspended. Gray hovered close behind her, and she felt his arms going around her.

"Don't, please," she asked him. Gray lowered his hands but remained close to her. "You don't believe any of this, do you? To you, this is all just bio-etheric energy, isn't it?"

Gray sighed. "You're asking me if I believe that all life, even the Earth itself, has a living spirit. And that we are all born from, and return to, this Gaia? I just . . . don't know, Aki."

He put his arms around her, though she tried to resist his strong embrace. Gently he touched the containment device on her chest. "Is this why you shut me out? You should have told me."

"I don't know how much time I have left," she admitted.

"Who does?"

For a moment, he moved closer, and it was tempting to kiss him. Then the gondola jolted back into life, and Aki staggered away from him. She quickly returned to the array of sensors. "Uh, I better get back to scanning."

Gray frowned, his dark eyes looking troubled. He turned to one of the windows and watched the shimmer of bio-etheric energy on the Barrier.

* * *

The next day, Captain Edwards was still troubled by Aki's rejection, but he had other problems. He'd been summoned to appear before General Hein himself. When he walked into Hein's office, he was first met by a stern-faced major. The general stood at the window, looking at the endless twilight that protected them from the Phantoms.

After they saluted, the major said, "Captain Edwards, you extracted a Dr. Ross from Old New York several days ago, did you not?"

"Yes, sir," answered Gray crisply.

"What were your impressions of Dr. Ross?" asked the major.

"She seemed very capable and determined, sir," answered the soldier.

The major nodded and glanced at the general. "You and the Deep Eyes are being temporarily reassigned. You will guard Dr. Ross when she reenters the wasteland."

"Understood, sir."

General Hein broke in, "You don't understand yet, Captain. Report any aberrant behavior in Dr. Ross to the major immediately."

"Aberrant behavior, sir?" asked Gray, trying to stay calm.

Hein whirled around. "The woman carries an alien infestation, Captain. We don't know what it may be doing to her. The alien presence could be affecting her judgment. They may be manipulating the doctor for their very own purposes."

"Is the general suggesting that Dr. Ross is a spy?" asked Gray evenly.

Hein sneered. "The general is wondering why he's explaining himself to a captain."

The major jumped in to explain, "She's had prolonged exposure to Phantom tissue. If this begins to manifest itself, in any way, Dr. Ross is to be placed under arrest and transported here for observation."

Gray felt Hein's uncomfortable gaze. The general was sizing him up, trying to decide where his loyalties lay. Maybe he already knew.

"It is, in fact, for her own good, Captain," said Hein with a sniff.

"Of course, sir," answered Gray, although neither one of them sounded convinced. The captain quickly saluted and marched out the door before he

CHAPTER 6

With screams, moans, and slashing sounds, the alien armies clashed on the barren plain. Aki stood among them, witnessing the carnage. She wanted to help or to run, but she was frozen by the awful sights and sounds. Hundreds died every minute on the bloody battlefield.

Suddenly, the aliens stopped fighting, and they rose to full height, towering above her. In unison, they turned to look at the human in their midst. This was more frightening than their battle, until Aki realized that they were looking past her . . . at the ravaged horizon.

The Deep Eyes were flying over the pock-marked, alien terrain—the same one from her dream. Aki felt as if her sleeping life and real life were beginning to merge. *I'm convinced that these dreams are some form of communication,* she thought. *The message still eludes me, but the dream is coming faster now and that can only mean one thing—*

The Phantoms inside me are beginning to win.

* * *

When Aki woke up, she found herself on the Deep Eyes troop transport, but they were not flying over the alien wasteland. They were flying over another wasteland—a battleground in the Arizona desert.

"Our target is fifty klicks west of Tucson," Jane was saying as she worked the navigation controls.

"Roger," said Neil from the cockpit. He was flying the craft while Ryan and Gray watched the scans from the surface. Jane's attention was focused on an abandoned cargo container on the surface.

"Phantom concentration?" asked Gray.

She gave him a grave look. "Not good. We've got big metas everywhere."

"So it's gonna be a real picnic," muttered Ryan.

The captain nodded. "Basic fire ineffective. Build up your charges and make them count."

He looked at Aki and mustered a wan smile.

"Stick close to me. No heroics today, okay? Everything by the book."

"By the book. Right," she answered.

Before he could respond, Jane began pointing out spots on her holographic map. "If we drop energy buoys here, here, and here . . . we should be able to land, acquire the target, and get out before the Phantoms even know we were there."

"And the buoys will attract the Phantoms?" asked Aki.

"Yeah," answered Jane.

"For a while," added Gray.

After that, conversation fell off. Aki began to notice the three new soldiers who sat across from them. These three kept their masks on, as if they were ready to fight at any moment.

Ryan noticed them, too, and he asked, "So, you're from the 307s, right? Under General Hein? Ever done any wasteland recon before? It can get pretty ugly."

They didn't answer. *Maybe they're afraid,* thought Aki. *Or maybe they've done recon and don't want to talk about it.* At any rate, silence took over for the rest of the ride.

Finally the troop transport dropped out of the clouds and skimmed over the ravaged desert. From its bomber bay, the ship began to drop the ovo-buoys. These large ovo-pacs floated down, stuck in the dirt, and released a haze of energy particles. No sooner did the first one detonate than a huge serpentine Phantom raced toward it. Metas, soldiers, flying Phantoms—they were all visible in the energy field.

The craft streaked past the decoy buoys and headed toward the blackened battleground. Twisted tanks, planes, Jeeps, and missiles lay crumpled and broken like old toys. Skeletons lay drying in the heat. *It looks like a graveyard,* thought Aki, *where no one bothered to bury the dead.*

Shooting thrusters and dust, the transport landed in the middle of this grim scene. The hatch popped open, and the Deep Eyes filed out in full armor and eyescopes. Her own breathing pounded in her ears as Aki followed after them. She could see Phantoms swarming around the nearest buoy.

"Looks like they've taken the bait," said Gray, his voice booming in her eyescope.

Aki watched the Phantoms with wonder, having never seen such a large variety of them. From this distance, she could easily see the big ones—the metas—but there were smaller ones, too. They had shapes like animals, and they teemed around the ovo-pacs like sharks in a feeding frenzy.

Gray signaled for the others to follow him, and

the Deep Eyes spread out in a line. As ordered, Aki stayed close to the captain. She checked her wrist scanner and pointed to a hill littered with twisted machines.

"The seventh spirit should be just beyond that line of wreckage," she reported.

"I don't see how any living thing could survive out here," said Gray.

"We'll find out soon enough." Aki led the way up the hill and through the wreckage. When she saw what was on the other side, she wished she had waited for the others. The battlefield was covered with dead soldiers. After ten years, they were nothing but skeletons and a bit of dried flesh.

As far as she could see, there was nothing but death—young lives snuffed out too quickly. Rusted machines and the remains of ovo-pac decoys were scattered among the corpses.

The Deep Eyes caught up with her, and they went silently down the hill together. It was slow going in the rugged terrain, skeletal remains, and dense wreckage.

"This was the 'Phantom Cleansing' mission," Ryan finally said. "It was supposed to end the war. My father's in here somewhere."

In the wake of that revelation, Aki's scanner

began to beep, and she quickened her step. "All right, let's move out, people," Gray ordered.

The deeper they walked into the carnage, the more depressing it was. Finally the indicator pointed upward, and Aki looked up from the devastation with relief. She saw a large hawk gliding overhead. All of them looked up at the same time, blinking their eyes in amazement. No, it wasn't a Phantom—it was a real bird.

"I'll be," said Ryan.

"A survivor," remarked Aki. "Hoping for life to return."

"Is that our spirit, Doc?" asked Ryan.

"No," she admitted sadly.

They passed more fallen soldiers, their skeletal arms frozen while reaching for the sky. In the distance, Phantoms danced on the horizon, still attracted by the ovo-buoys. They seemed to be massing in frightening numbers.

"We're closing in on the life form," reported Aki.

"Distance?" asked Gray uneasily.

Aki checked her wrist scanner and muttered, "Hard to say. We're very close." She felt a slight pain in her chest, but hoped it was just nerves.

"I don't see anything," said Gray.

Neither did Aki, who was using her eyes as well as her instruments to scan the killing field. All she

saw was more bones, and the beeping led her to one in particular—

"You're not gonna tell me it's *him?*" asked Gray in confusion. The captain turned over the body, and a skull dropped out of the rusted helmet. The man's armor fell away like the shell of a broken egg. Startled, Gray dropped the corpse and stepped back. Aki's scanner kept beeping insistently. She adjusted the scope for minute detail of the corpse.

"It's not the soldier," said Aki quickly. "It's his ovo-pac."

Gray stared at the dead man's backpack. "How do you explain that? The pacs power our weapons, the Barrier cities. I mean, it's just bio-etheric energy."

"And to create that energy we use living tissue," said Aki excitedly. "Single cell organisms!"

"You're telling me his backpack is the seventh spirit?" asked Gray incredulously.

"Yes."

With a burst of static, Neil's voice came over the comm system. "Do you read me, Captain? We have incoming!"

Aki and Gray looked up to see Phantoms loping and writhing toward them from every direction. They vaulted the wreckage and slithered over the dead bodies. Aki whirled in another direction, only to see a huge Phantom drop from the sky. It lashed at one of the new Deep Eyes and ripped the spirit right out of his body.

The discharged energy bathed them both in an eerie light. Then the soldier's spirit and the Phantom diffused into light particles, as they had canceled each other out. The lifeless body of the 307 just dropped to the ground, joining thousands of others.

The Deep Eyes drew their weapons and began to fire at the advancing horde.

"Ryan, get the soldier's pack!" ordered Gray. At once, the soldier moved to retrieve the ovo-pac from the long-dead skeleton.

"Those buoys . . . they're not working," said Aki in alarm. She clutched her stomach, feeling nauseous.

"Thank you," muttered Gray at the obvious statement. "Are you all right?"

Trying not to show how sick she felt, Aki nodded. "Of course I am."

Ryan rushed past with the ovo-pac, while the other Deep Eyes kept firing. "Let's get outta here!" shouted Gray. Soon the Deep Eyes were in a controlled retreat, firing at the Phantoms as they backed toward the transport.

"Something's not right," yelled Jane. Her energy beam swept a wrecked tank and blasted three Phantoms to bits. "This shouldn't be happening!"

"Something's attracting them!" agreed Ryan.

Aki saw Jane looking intensely at her, while the others glanced in her direction. It was all Aki could do to stay on her feet, she felt so ill. She staggered a few more steps and was about to fall when Gray grabbed her and held her up. Even though his face was covered by his mask, she could sense his sympathy . . . and fear.

As the Phantoms swooped closer, Jane shouted, "They're right on us, sir! Closing in fast."

"Jane, take the lead!" ordered the captain. He lifted Aki's limp body and began to run. All she could see were glowing Phantoms everywhere— writhing, teeming, leaping over the ruins. They were right on the heels of the Deep Eyes.

"Fire in the hole!" shouted Jane.

Suddenly, a tremendous explosion shook the ground, and the air rippled with bio-etheric energy. *It's almost like my dream!* That was the last thing Aki remembered before she passed out in the captain's arms.

CHAPTER 7

On the troop transport, Captain Edwards cradled Aki in his arms, uncertain what to do. For the moment, he couldn't do anything for her—the only one who could save them was their pilot. Gray looked out the window in time to see a huge serpentine Phantom streaking toward the tiny craft.

In the cockpit, Neil worked feverishly on the holographic controls. The ship veered to the left, narrowly missing the hideous Phantom, but they swiftly faced another monster rising from below.

With a quick maneuver, Neil changed course, and they swerved away from the glittering maw of the Phantom's mouth. But before anyone could celebrate, the transport careened into a rock wall. Rocks thudded on the hull of the transport, causing all of them to catch their breath.

Luckily the transport held together. With grim determination, Neil put them into a fast climb. The transport roared away from the scarred battlefield, which swarmed with ghostly shapes.

Now Gray had a moment to attend to Aki. He placed her on a field gurney and activated the holographic display. He didn't need to be a medic to know that she was bad—he had seen that infestation before. But with her prototype containment field, he didn't know how he should proceed. One false step, and he could kill her.

"We have to get her to a hospital," Gray announced.

A soldier, one of the new 307s, gazed up at him. "You have your orders, sir."

His fellow spy suddenly lifted his gun, aiming old-fashioned bullets at the Deep Eyes. His grim expressions made it clear they were serious.

"What's going on here?" demanded the captain.

"Dr. Ross is to be taken into custody now, sir," said the lead 307. When Jane and Ryan moved to resist, the 307s took aim at them. Everyone was taken by surprise.

Neil looked back nervously from the cockpit, and the captain gave him a look that told him to keep flying. Then he turned back to the strangers and barked, "Lower your weapons. That's an order!"

"I'm sorry, sir. We have no choice but to relieve you of your command," said the stone-faced traitor, never moving his gun barrel from Gray's chest.

The big man scowled. "I won't let you do this, soldier. You're going to have to shoot me."

"Stand down, Captain!" ordered the stranger.

* * *

Aki was in her own private world—her dream. Once again, she was surrounded by thousands of battling aliens. Only this time they had stopped fighting and were waiting, just as she waited. Most of them towered above Aki, their bizarre tentacles and appendages shuffling in the red dirt.

Suddenly Aki heard a roar that was worse than the two shrieking armies. She whirled around to see a wall of fire scorching the barren land. The inferno burned dirt, stumps, and ruins alike, as it raced straight toward her. Aki barely had time to throw her hands up and scream—

* * *

When Aki screamed in the gondola, her action so startled the spies that one of them fired his weapon. The bullet pierced her chest plate, and Aki was hurled back into her seat. Gray scowled angrily, but he did nothing—he could see Jane moving while their attention was diverted.

She leaped over the chair and was on the solider in a flash. Jane kicked away his weapon, while she finished him with a right hook to the jaw.

That all happened in an instant. Gray turned back to Aki. Sick and now shot . . . she had to be near death! All the captain could do was cradle her and try to protect her during the action.

Ryan got into the fight, grappling with the other 307. Neil was doing his best to help his mates by flying the shuttle like a madman and dumping everyone back and forth in the cabin. The captain was alarmed when he saw Phantoms out the window, coming dangerously close. They were headed back to the battlefield!

One of the idiot 307s fired his weapon, and everyone scrambled for cover. Suddenly a voice shouted, "That's enough! Hands where I can see them. Everyone! *Now!*"

Gray was soon staring down a gun barrel, and it was clear that one of the traitors had gotten control. The captain clutched Aki in his arms, making it obvious where his loyalties lay.

Without warning, a Phantom oozed through the hull of the transport and whipped through the man with the gun. His brilliant blue spirit was snatched from his body, and it hung in the air like smoke over a campfire. His armor kept his body upright for a moment, but the soldier finally crumpled to the deck, dead.

Everyone froze in horror, except for Neil, who quickly sent the craft climbing again. The Deep Eyes subdued the last 307 and regained control of their transport, but Aki was in terrible shape. Gray peered at her chest plate, where he could see the vibrant Phantom infestation. Had it gotten worse?

After a little more probing and searching, he found the bullet lodged in the containment device. He fought the impulse to take it out, because the gizmo was still working. There was only one person who could fix that machine and keep her alive.

"Neil, get us back to New York!" he ordered. "Fast!"

* * *

When General Hein heard about the unlucky mission, he rubbed his hands together with delight. "Issue an order. I want Captain Edwards and Dr. Ross placed under arrest. All research materials pertaining to Dr. Sid's wave theory are to be confiscated immediately."

"That might not go over too well with the Council, sir," said the major.

The general rose to his feet and nodded with satisfaction. "Ah, what a tragedy that would be. No. This is what I've been waiting for. The good captain has opened the door for us. By tomorrow morning, the Council will be at our feet, thanking us for exposing the traitors in our midst . . . and imploring us to save them from the Phantoms."

General Hein began to pace, deep in thought. There was much to be done before they begged him for help.

CHAPTER 8

Gray rushed Aki into the treatment center, carrying the fallen scientist in his arms. Sid met them, and the doctor guided the captain to the operating table. Medical assistants hovered nearby, and as soon as he placed Aki on the table, they took over.

"How is she, Doctor?" asked Gray worriedly.

The old man shook his head. "She is dying."

"But there must be *something* you can do."

With a gulp, the doctor opened Aki's tunic to reveal the containment device attached to her chest. It was still working, but all the readouts looked alarmingly high.

"Aki is fighting with only six of the eight spirits," reported Sid. "We'll have to implant the seventh directly into her chest plate."

"It took a bullet," said Gray. "I think it might be damaged."

Sid searched for the bullet and found it, then his frown deepened. "We have to repair this panel quickly."

The doctor motioned to his assistants, and they flew into action. Gray glanced at his fellow Deep Eyes in the back of the room, then turned his gaze to Aki. It was scary to see her so helpless, so close to death. He hovered nearby, wondering how he could help.

Sid conferred with his assistants for a moment, then he took the captain aside. "Her vital signs are dropping," he began, "Aki is slipping away from us. She needs a sympathetic spirit to help hold her in this world, and I can think of no spirit better suited for that task than yours, Captain."

Before Gray's worried mind could process that, the medical assistants were leading him toward another operating table. The captain turned around. "I don't understand—"

"You don't have to understand," answered Sid, laying a comforting hand on the captain's shoulder. "You just be with her now. You keep her here with us."

The rest was a mass of confusion, as Gray was stretched out on the operating table and people hovered around him. The doctor talked to the Deep Eyes in the corner, while his assistants moved the captain's bed next to Aki. He reached over and took her hand, and that simple action transported him to a strange, alien vista. . . .

The land was blasted, eroded, and ugly—miles and miles of gnarled badlands. The only beautiful thing was Aki, standing beside him. Gray warmly squeezed her hand.

"Aki, where are we?" he asked in confusion.

"On an alien planet," she answered evenly.

"How is that possible?"

"I'm not entirely sure." She kicked a blood-red stone on the ground, and they listened to it clatter in the reddish dust.

"You seem pretty calm," said Gray.

Aki shrugged. "I've been having this dream every night for months."

"Dream?"

"Well, whatever it is." She blinked in amazement at him. "You're really *here,* aren't you? What's happening to me?"

"Dr. Sid is implanting the seventh spirit directly into your body," answered Gray hesitantly.

Aki's lovely face lit up with a smile. "Then you're my spiritual support? Gray, how sweet of you!"

"Look, I don't think you realize how serious this situation is," said the captain gravely.

Despite his warning, Aki looked perfectly calm.

A warm breeze made Gray's close-cropped hair stand on end, and he knew something was about to happen. With a strange roar, the ground began to shake under his feet. An earthquake!

No, more like a stampede of thundering hooves, thought the soldier after a moment. *It's the rush of charging—of charging into battle!*

Gray looked up to see a rabid alien army come pouring over the horizon, blotting out the ruined wasteland. They looked like Phantoms, only now they were solid beings. He gripped Aki's hand and tried to pull her away—to run! She jerked out of his grasp and merely caught his hand. Her gaze asked him to remain calm, as if she wanted him to see this disturbing vision.

When a second army appeared behind them, Gray had no choice but to remain and let the battle swirl around him. The two monstrous hordes met on the field of battle, hacking and shooting, but somehow he and Aki remained untouched. Until suddenly . . .

The Phantom armies stopped their battle and stared at the two humans. Their faces looked like ghosts . . . or like memories. In their infinite variety, the towering aliens were horrible. *And yet beautiful.*

"W-what are they doing? Why are they staring at us?" asked Gray.

"Not at *us,*" answered Aki. She motioned behind

them, and Gray turned to see a monstrous wall of flame bearing down on them. The blaze swept over the wasteland, scorching everything in its path. The Phantom armies were vaporized where they stood, and their remains blew away like dust.

Gray and Aki remained untouched.

Then real earthquakes gripped the land, giant cracks split the ground, and crags shot up from the dirt. Burning lava and geysers spewed from the cracks, and it was clearly the end of this world. Gray and Aki were the only ones left to witness the upheaval, and he was grateful to have her calming influence near him in this strange vision.

The two of them floated in space, where they could watch the final destruction of the alien planet. It was breaking up into large chunks—meteors the size of moons. Outlined in the dust were the exiled spirits from the final battle. As a meteor broke off from the planet, these cursed spirits were sucked into it. Then the monstrous rock hurtled through space . . .

* * *

"Welcome back, Captain," said a voice from high above. With a start, Gray opened his eyes and glanced around the room. He was back in the treatment center, surrounded by Dr. Sid's equipment and workers. The great man himself came slowly into focus, and he was smiling.

"Is it over? How is she, Doctor?" asked Gray urgently. He glanced at Aki, who was sleeping peacefully beside him.

"She's going to be fine," said the doctor. "But this is only temporary. We'll need to find the eighth and final spirit to cure her."

Gray nodded, telling himself to be patient. He leaned over and gently touched the young woman's cheek. "Aki? Can you hear me?"

Slowly she began to stir, then Aki blinked awake. She smiled when she saw Gray, and he grinned back. Although she looked weak and pale, she beamed with happiness.

"I finished it," said Aki with relief. "I know what it means. I know what the Phantoms really are—"

Before she could finish, the doors at the front and rear of the treatment center banged open, and military police poured into the room. Gray tried to sit up to resist them, but he was very weak, too. He could only watch as General Hein's soldiers surrounded them. They were dressed in full battle gear and carrying serious weaponry. The Deep Eyes had to back down.

"Nobody move!" ordered the lead MP. "You are all under arrest!"

CHAPTER 9

General Hein sat in his private office, gazing out the window at the city of San Francisco. Even from this distance, it looked cold, dead, drained of life—a massive tombstone.

Gritting his teeth, the general turned to look at the special force he had assembled. Standing before him were his most loyal officers and toughest soldiers. These were the ones who had proven themselves in battle—the ones who had proven they hated Phantoms.

His chief aide put down his radio and smiled. "We have them, sir." General Hein said nothing—he was deep in thought, planning the annihilation of the Phantoms.

"Sir?" asked the major, trying to get his attention.

"My wife and daughter were killed by Phantoms

when the San Francisco Barrier city was attacked," said the general, looking out the window. "Did I ever tell you that?"

The major nodded that he had, but the general went on. "I try to imagine what that must've been like, seeing everyone around you fall over dead for no apparent reason. And then, at the end, feeling something next to you, invisible, touching you, reaching inside your body and—"

With a shudder, the general got control of himself. "You've lost family, haven't you?"

"Y-yes, sir," answered the major quickly.

Hein turned to the soldiers. "That's why I trust you, all of you. You know what must be done."

These soldiers will not let me down, thought Hein. *It will be easy to discredit Dr. Sid and Aki Ross, now that we have Aki's dream records.* Those two were clearly traitors, and so was the captain who wouldn't obey orders. But all of that might not be enough to get the Council to let him use the Zeus Cannon.

No, he would need a real threat.

* * *

Ten minutes later, General Hein, the major, and a hand-picked squad of soldiers were in an elevator, moving through the facility which housed the enormous generators necessary to maintain the Barrier. It was the humans' only defense against the Phantoms. They passed massive machinery, hydraulic pumps, and gleaming green ovo-tubes.

An impressive place, thought Hein, but it was outdated. It only held the invaders at bay. They had to get away from containment and embrace total destruction of the enemy.

The team finally reached the bottom of the Barrier Generator Facility, where a handful of technicians ran the instruments. The general strode across the floor, while his soldiers fanned out around the workers. Before they knew it, each technician had a gun barrel in his face.

"Major, arrest these men!" ordered the general. He strode toward the massive ovo-tank in the center of the room and looked at the blinking display. It was here that the bio-etheric energy was produced and stored to create the Barrier.

In a few seconds, the technicians were forced onto the elevator, and Hein's squad moved in. Soon there was a soldier at every station, and others standing guard. Hein saw the major at the master controls, and he stepped to his side.

"Reduce power to Sector 31," he ordered the major.

The officer gaped at him. "Sir . . . you do realize that the Phantoms will—"

"What I realize, Major, is that we must force the Council to take action against the enemy." General Hein glared at the underlings until his order was followed.

"Twenty-five percent of energy pipe alpha redirected," reported one soldier.

"Lowering power output to Sector 31," said another.

The general moved to a security monitor offering a view of the Barrier outside. He watched for any changes, and his patience was soon rewarded. A small section of the Barrier faded slightly, then there was a bright discharge. In a flash, an alien tentacle shot from the shadows, writhing hysterically.

More glittering appendages followed, and soon there were a dozen writhing tentacles moving through the breach in the Barrier.

The major broke in, "Barrier breach in Sector 31, General. They're coming through now."

Hein turned, not wanting the major to see the smile on his face. "Oh, I think we can easily handle a few Phantoms in a contained space. Relax, Major. When this night's over, you're going to be a hero."

* * *

Captain Edwards paced the length of the cell, where he was confined with Aki and Dr. Sid. In another cell, Ryan, Jane, and Neil cooled their heels. Gleaming red laser beams protected the door from any attempt to escape. Aki watched Gray while he paced. The captain had shared her dreams and her spirits, and he was giving her a new reason to live.

Still she felt sorry for Gray, because he had to absorb so much. This war wasn't about science and weapons, it was about the spirits within. Gray, Jane, Neil, and Ryan couldn't understand how they had ended up in a military prison, but Aki knew why. Some powerful people didn't want to face the true nature of this war.

Gray stopped pacing long enough to shake his head. "Aki, I don't think—"

"You were there, Gray," she said evenly. "You saw it."

"That's just it. I'm not sure what I saw. How can you be?" Gray started pacing again.

"Captain, please let her continue," replied Sid.

"All right." Aki wracked her brain for an example they would understand. "Why do you think we've never been able to determine a relationship between the human-sized Phantoms and the giant ones roaming the wastelands?"

"Excuse me, Doc," said Neil, breaking in. "But what friggin' relationship? I mean, you got your human-size Phantoms, a-a-and your creepy cater-pillary Phantoms, and your flying Phantoms. And let's not forget my personal favorite, the big, fat, giant Phantoms!"

"Down, boy," ordered Jane.

"He's right," said Ryan. "If you've spent as much time in the field as we have, you know there *is* no relationship. It's like a zoo out there."

"Precisely. I think those giant ones are like our whales or elephants." Aki looked at the Deep Eyes, begging for understanding.

Neil scratched his head. "Why would an invading army bring a bunch of whales and elephants along for the ride? Unless their ship was some kind of crazy Noah's Ark?"

"Well," answered Sid, "we have always assumed the meteor was intended as a form of transporta-tion. Perhaps it wasn't."

Aki nodded in agreement. "The meteor is a chunk of their planet that got hurled into space when they destroyed their own world."

The Deep Eyes looked at one another in confu-sion, and Neil blurted, "But . . . how could they sur-vive the trip across outer space on a hunk of rock?"

"They didn't," answered Aki sadly.

"Huh?" asked Neil. "This is all beginning to make a creepy kinda sense. What do *you* think, Captain?"

"I think that explains why we never had a chance," answered Gray. "All our strategies are based on one assumption: that we were fighting alien invaders."

Aki looked grateful for his understanding. "Think of the dream, Gray. How they died. Since then, all they've known is suffering.

"They're not an invading army—they're ghosts."

* * *

General Hein looked with satisfaction at the situation map in the Barrier Control Center. It was lit up with dozens of blazing dots, signifying Phantom incursions. The major stood at the controls, scanning the Barrier over New York.

"Excellent," crowed General Hein. "Sound an alert. Send a squad out to eliminate them."

"Sir? I have numerous Phantom contacts!" said a soldier on another station.

"Well, of course you do."

"Outside of Sector 31, sir! And moving at incredible speed!"

Hein strode to his position and looked at his holographic screen. The red blips were moving through the city almost faster than the scanners could catch them. "Major, what is going on here?" demanded the general.

Grim-faced, the major checked his own readouts. "They're in the pipes. They're moving with the bio-etheric energy flow."

"That's impossible," muttered Hein. "No living thing could survive in those pipes."

The major's eyes widened with horror. "We've got a big one heading this way, sir!"

Everyone in the room looked up at the huge overhead pipes, pulsating with their greenish energy flow. Within one pipe appeared an ominous black shape. The soldiers groped for their weapons and pulled on their helmets, preparing to do battle.

"Oh, my God," muttered Hein. When he looked at his men, he realized they were about to fire at the precious ovo-pipes, which would destroy them all. "Hold your fire!"

The snakelike Phantom suddenly stuck its head out of the central ovo-tank and swallowed up the nearest soldier. The terrified men began to fire, despite the general's warning. The big ovo-tank glowed brightly for a moment before it exploded, and the entire room was ripped by a chain reaction of devastating explosions.

The major stared at the general in panic, but

there was nothing to be done. "We've got to get to the Zeus Station!" shouted Hein.

The two officers turned on their heels and ran for their lives.

All across the ravaged planet, ovo-pacs and tubes exploded. One by one, the great Barriers, which separated the humans from the Phantoms, began to disappear.

* * *

In the military cell, the prisoners waited forlornly for their fate. Aki felt badly for Gray and the Deep Eyes, but she felt worse for Sid. He had been so close to finding the eighth and final spirit—and to achieving proof of the existence of the Gaia spirit.

Gray paced restlessly. "Come on, Neil, we need to find a way out. Now you're our man . . . think!"

"Captain," said the soldier helplessly, "these walls are titanium alloy, and the bars are pulse-sonic lasers. I mean it's not like I can just wave a magic wand and . . . whoa!"

Without warning, the lights flickered, and the cell door popped open. Everyone jumped to their feet and looked around uneasily. No guards had entered, and there was no one around. Was this some kind of trap?

"Neil, I'm impressed," said Gray quietly.

"That makes two of us," answered the young soldier.

Before anyone could say anything else, a computer voice broke in. "Proceed to the nearest evacuation facility. Proceed to the nearest evacuation facility."

"I think we should proceed to the nearest evacuation facility," said Neil, stepping out of the cell.

Gray turned to Aki, then he motioned to the others to follow him. The four Deep Eyes and the two scientists dashed through a prison that was now strangely open and deserted. As they stepped out of the main gate, they found themselves on a balcony above the street. Below them, it was mass panic.

People were running everywhere, trying to escape, and it wasn't hard to see why. The Barrier was flickering, and hundreds of Phantoms were visible as they poured through into the realm of the living.

CHAPTER 10

On the street below them, the Phantoms mercilessly attacked the fleeing people. The shimmering aliens stole their spirits, lifting them above their heads. Dozens of corpses collapsed to the ground. Phantoms oozed through the weakened Barrier, from the concrete, from the buildings. They were everywhere!

Aki, Gray, Sid, and the Deep Eyes stood on the ramparts of the military prison, watching the monstrous scene unfold. Aki wanted to run, but where was there to go? Without warning, a huge Phantom emerged through the balcony, separating her and Gray from the others. The captain grabbed her arm and pulled her away.

The two of them began to run down the deserted

corridor. "What about the others?" shouted Aki. "Dr. Sid!"

"The Deep Eyes will take care of him," answered Gray, tugging on her arm. "Come on!"

They dashed to the elevator, and Gray pounded on the down button. Ghostly Phantoms floated through the hallway, coming closer, and Aki dug her fingernails into Gray's arm. At the last moment, the elevator opened, and they jumped inside. Colorful tentacles slithered through the door, snapping at them, but the elevator car moved faster than the Phantoms.

Aki slumped against the wall, out of breath. "How come we can see them now?"

"They must be carrying a residual charge from passing through the Barrier," answered Gray. "With luck, we can make the monorail."

When they reached the underground monorail station, they were horrified to find bodies littering the platform. The door of one monorail car tried to shut, but there were too many bodies in the way. A computer voice intoned, "Trains are not operating. We apologize for the inconvenience."

They stepped over the bodies, trying to get to the car, but Phantoms rose from the platform. Within seconds, they were completely surrounded by shimmering apparitions. There was no escape. Gray gripped her shoulders tightly, and his grim expression told her that this was the end of the line.

Suddenly there was a loud crash, and an armored vehicle blasted through a storefront. It looked like a convertible Hummer with the top down. The vehicle came rumbling down the platform, headed straight toward them. Ryan and Jane leaned out of the windows, firing at the howling Phantoms. Neil was behind the wheel, and Aki could see Dr. Sid seated beside him.

They slowed down just long enough for Aki and Gray to jump aboard. With Neil flooring the accelerator, the armored car roared down the tunnel.

As Aki slumped into a seat, Jane gave her a grim smile. "What now?"

"We need to find my ship," answered the scientist, thinking of the shuttlecraft she had been forced to abandon a few days ago, when searching for the sixth spirit.

"If it was towed inside the city, it would be in the military hangar," said Ryan.

"That's a big 'if,' " muttered Neil.

A moment later, the armored car burst from the tunnel into the street, where it was still chaotic. Some people had grabbed escape pods, but most of the pods couldn't be launched fast enough. The Phantoms ripped into them like bullets hitting old

"The dream is always the same."
—*Aki*

The Barrier City

Inside the scanning chamber

Phantom infestation

Neil

Jane

"You may have bought us some time, Aki, but I wonder—at what cost?"

—*Sid*

Ryan

LOCATED   The Seventh Spirit

The battlefield ruins

"We have incoming . . .
Do you read me . . . ?"
—*Neil*

Phantoms!

The
transporter

"Let me do this, Aki. Trust me . . .
Don't back out on me . . . now that I
finally believe . . . I love you."
—*Gray*

tin cans. There was screaming and panic everywhere.

At that moment, an escape pod crashed through a wall right in front of them—with people clinging to it. Neil swerved the vehicle to barely miss the pod, and they plowed down a passageway between two buildings.

They managed to drive in silence for several minutes, as the city fell apart all around them. Aki glanced out the window and saw a sign pointing to the airport. Suddenly a huge meta-Phantom slithered in their way.

"Over the ramp!" ordered Gray. "We're going through the station!"

He pointed to a metal ramp that led to open space over the highway, with a building just beyond it. The Deep Eyes tried to tell him he was crazy, but the captain looked determined. Besides, there was no other way out.

"Hang on, everybody!" shouted Neil. With a spin of the steering wheel, he sent the armored car rumbling up the ramp. A moment later, they were airborne, and Aki looked down to see the street far below them.

A moment later, they crashed through a wall of glass, and Aki was tossed to the floor. With a groan of stressed metal, the car finally came to rest on a pile of rubble, its wheels spinning helplessly.

Aki could hardly see anything in the smoke and sparks, but she heard voices. "Doc?" said Neil. "Are you all right?"

Sid lifted his head from under the wrecked dashboard, his eyes wide with fright. "Interesting," he murmured.

"Anybody hurt?" asked Gray.

"Captain!" called Jane with concern.

Aki turned around to see Ryan in the back of the vehicle. He was pinned under a chunk of metal, and what looked like an axle stuck from his abdomen. She didn't need any medical instruments to know it was bad.

"Oh, God!" groaned Neil. "Talk to me, Sarge."

The wounded soldier put on a brave face and said, "Ouch."

Neil scrambled back toward his friend, and they tried to lift the wreckage that was pinning him. *But what can we do about that chunk of metal in his abdomen?* thought Aki.

"Gimme a hand, Jane," Neil said.

"No, wait," ordered Sid. "We're risking further injury. We need the proper tools to cut him out."

Aki reached into her belt pouch for a hypodermic syringe, which she carried to treat herself. "I have what we need in my ship."

Ryan waved off the syringe and groaned. "No, Doc. No drugs."

Sid looked curiously at Gray. "Captain?"

"You heard the man." Gray picked up a weapon and checked the charge. "We'll find the ship and be back for you."

"I'll stay with you," said Jane.

"Me, too," replied Neil.

"Nobody's staying," said the wounded man. "Just give me a gun."

Everyone looked at the captain for a decision. He finally nodded and said, "You got it. Jane, give him a weapon."

When she hesitated, Gray barked, "Do it!"

Holding back her tears, the hardened soldier gave Ryan the biggest weapon they had. Gray opened the door and pulled himself out. "We'll be back for you, Sergeant. You *hear* me?"

Ryan nodded bravely. "I hear you, Captain. Now get outta here."

A moment later, Aki, Gray, Sid, Neil, and Jane were dashing across a deserted airport runway. Debris from crashed escape pods was strewn everywhere, and smoke drifted across the night sky. Aki could hear the sound of gunfire, and she glanced back to where they had left the sergeant.

Gray gave her a push and kept her moving. She

was glad he did, because a welcome shape loomed in the distance. It was the sleek black hull of her beloved shuttlecraft, the *Black Boa*. As soon as she reached the craft, she began to operate the access panel. A gangway descended from the underbelly of the small craft, and all of them staggered aboard.

They found themselves in the cargo bay, where there was a small Quatro land rover. Neil immediately went to the tiny vehicle and grinned. "A quad-axle ATV. This is good."

"It can be used to retrieve Ryan and transport him safely here," said Dr. Sid. He bent down and pulled out the vehicle's gel packs. "However, we'll need to replace these spent fuel cells."

"There could be some live ovo-pacs in the hangar," said Jane.

"All right," said Gray, taking charge. "Jane, check the hangar. Neil, get us ready for takeoff. Aki and Dr. Sid, prep the Quatro. I'll go to the tower and rotate the airtray. This city may be lost, but we are not. Let's do this thing and get out of here."

As the rest of them dispersed to do their jobs, Aki turned to the captain. "Gray, be careful."

"You, too," he answered with a smile.

* * *

"Darn it," said Neil from the cockpit of the *Black Boa*. He tapped his radio headpiece. "*Black Boa* to control tower. Stop the airtray, Captain. We have a problem. I'm reading an impound tractor still attached to the prow of the ship."

This was a royal pain, because everything else was going so smoothly. Jane had found plenty of fresh ovo-pacs, and the two scientists had gotten the Quatro moving. The captain was in the control tower, activating the airtray to move the *Black Boa* into launch position. The shuttlecraft checked out on all systems and was ready to go, except for the impound tractor holding it down.

Gray's voice came back, "We can't take off like that."

"Permission to go outside and detach the coupling," said Neil.

After a moment, the captain replied, "Do it."

Jane stuck her head into the cockpit. "What's the problem?"

"Ah, we're locked down. I gotta go back out and uncouple the ship."

"I'm coming with you," declared Jane, belting on her ammo pack.

A moment later, the two of them were standing outside in the chill night air, inspecting a bootlike device placed on the nose of the shuttlecraft. Neil bent down and started to rewire the mechanism, while Jane hefted her weapon and nervously surveyed the dark horizon.

"The controls are locked, naturally," grumbled the soldier as he worked. "Jane, let me ask you something."

The female soldier twitched nervously and lifted her rifle. Something had caught her eye on the outer perimeter.

"You think we're gonna get out of here alive?" asked Neil. Jane didn't answer, but he kept on talking as he worked. It helped to calm his nerves. "I mean, I wonder if anybody else has gotten out. You think anyone made it this far? Huh?"

She muttered something, never taking her eyes off the runway. So Neil went on, "You think this 'eighth spirit' stuff is really gonna work against the Phantoms? I mean, what if it's all just a bunch of mumbo-jumbo?"

He crossed two wires, and the device sparked, giving him a shock. "Yeoww! Jane, do you mind if we stop talking? I'm trying to concentrate here."

By way of answer, she lifted her weapon and began to fire into the darkness, which could only mean one thing. The Phantoms had found them.

The captain's voice crackled on the radio. "What's happening down there?"

"Nothing we can't handle," responded Jane.

"Neil, what's your status?" asked Gray.

He gritted his teeth and hurried his fingers. "Almost there."

"I want you two back inside."

"We're fine, sir," answered Neil. "Jane is negotiating with extreme prejudice."

"No problem here, Captain," she said, ripping the night with colorful beams. Neil was too busy to look at her targets, but he could imagine what they were. Suddenly, the coupling clicked and fell off the wheel.

"Yes!" crowed Neil, rising to his feet. "Captain, we are good to go!"

He looked at Jane, expecting to see a happy grin on her face. Instead there was a look of sheer horror as she stared at him. Neil couldn't figure out what had spooked her so badly, until he followed her eyes and looked down at his own chest.

Two blazing tentacles protruded from his chest, and they were writhing in triumph. There was no pain, just darkness, which swiftly swept over his mind.

Neil was dead before he hit the concrete.

CHAPTER II

In the cargo bay of the *Black Boa,* Aki and Sid could hear the frantic voice of Captain Edwards. "Jane, get out of there! Get out of there *now!* Go! Jane! Get outta there!"

Aki jumped out of the Quatro and rushed to a viewport. She couldn't get a direct view of the nose of the shuttlecraft, but she could see the flashes of Jane's weapon . . . plus the ghostly swirl of Phantoms, closing in. She also felt movement—the airtray was slowly revolving. *Gray started the launch sequence!*

She rushed back to Sid, who was still in the Quatro. "I'm going to the cockpit. The ship is set on auto pilot. We're in countdown to lift-off." She knew the *Black Boa* would launch automatically once it was in position.

"But Gray is still in the control tower."

"I know," she answered grimly.

"We've got shields on the Quatro," protested Sid. "Out there . . . it's too dangerous! Aki!"

But she was already gone. As Aki ran down the corridor to the front of the ship, she could see Phantoms oozing through the bulkheads of the shuttle. *If we can just take off in time,* she thought, *we might be safe. But I'm not leaving without the others.*

Running as fast as she could, Aki reached the cockpit and dropped into her familiar seat. Phantoms flew all around them, rising from the runway, slipping in and out of the buildings. As the *Black Boa* slowly swiveled around on the airtray, the control tower came into view. A man was on the balcony, firing at the Phantoms, trying to keep them away from the shuttlecraft.

Gray—he's still alive! Another soldier staggered into view, also firing rapidly at the monsters. *Who was that?* It had to be the injured Ryan, who had come to help them. He fired into the hangar, which erupted in blazing green explosions.

With a jolt, the thrusters fired, and the *Black Boa* began to lift off the runway. Aki glanced back out the window to see a huge meta-Phantom swallow Ryan whole. Frantically, she banged on the radio. "Gray, do you read me? What's happening?"

"You and Sid are getting out of here now," he barked.

"No. We won't leave everyone!"

"Everyone's dead," he answered grimly.

"I'm not leaving without you!"

"I'm sorry . . . but you don't have a choice. Good-bye, Aki." With his words, the auto-pilot display disappeared, and Aki took manual control of the ship. A Phantom suddenly appeared beside her, and she gripped the lever and put the ship into a sharp bank, causing the hull to slip over the Phantom and leave it outside.

Aki piloted the shuttlecraft around the side of the control tower. There he was—one man battling a horde of Phantoms! With no time to spare, she opened the hatch and dropped the landing platform. Then she zoomed straight toward him.

"Gray!" she shouted into the radio. "Come on!"

As Phantoms twitched all around him, the captain leaped onto the platform and was whisked to safety. She retracted the mechanism back into the shuttlecraft, just as the cockpit filled with shimmering neon shapes.

At once, Aki slammed the thrusters on full, and the *Black Boa* roared away. One by one, the Phantoms were sucked out through the hull and into space. She glanced out the window and could see them floating toward the ground, like giant neon jellyfish.

A teardrop seeped from her eye. They were all dead—Ryan, Neil, and Jane, not to mention millions of people in New York. If the Barrier had fallen here, it must have fallen everywhere. Would there be anybody left to save?

* * *

In orbit over the Earth, Aki rested by her favorite window and stared down at the glistening blue planet. Gray floated beside her, not saying anything. His troubled expression told her everything she needed to know. They had clung to each other in their despair.

On the intercom, Sid's voice broke in. "You'd better come to the lab. I found the eighth spirit."

That broke them out of their stupor, and the two of them floated toward the *Black Boa*'s laboratory. They found the doctor bent over a holographic display, where he was combining spirit waves in a simulation. At last, he had the full blazing spectrum of wave patterns, and he looked satisfied.

"I enlarged the scanning perimeter to include an area that we had previously overlooked," explained Sid, bringing up a map.

Aki peered over his shoulder at the holographic chart and could hardly believe what she saw—the massive crater and remains of the Leonid meteor strike. "The impact crater?"

Gray frowned. "That's a strange place to find the eighth spirit."

"Yes," agreed Sid. "Really quite astonishing."

"But nothing could survive in there except Phantoms," said Gray.

The doctor nodded. "Precisely. Which suggests that the eighth spirit is a Phantom spirit. I can't explain it at the moment. But once we get down there—"

"Wait, Doctor," said Gray. "That's a one-way trip."

The old man sighed. "Yes, yes. I expected that's how you would evaluate our chances."

"Well, am I wrong?"

"No, no, no . . . I agree. We probably won't live long enough to extract the eighth spirit from the crater."

"Then why should we even try it?" asked Gray.

"Because we don't need to *extract* the eighth spirit!"

Aki nodded with understanding. "If we can't bring the final spirit here, we can go *there* and complete the wave inside the crater."

"Yes, exactly," agreed the doctor.

Gray still looked doubtful. "And how do we do that, exactly?"

"I can construct a device that would attach to Aki's chest plate to gather the eight spirits and then . . ."

"And then what?" asked Gray.

"And then, we wait and see what happens."

The soldier scowled with disbelief. "That's it? That's your plan? We 'wait and see what happens'? "

"Yes," answered Sid, looking hurt.

"Oh, good," snapped Gray. "Well, I got my own plan. We keep scanning the surface from orbit, and maybe we'll find a compatible spirit somewhere else."

The scientist looked at the young woman beside him. "Aki?"

She placed her hand inside the hologram, as if touching the glowing crater. "I say we go in."

* * *

General Hein tried not to show his relief as he floated off his shuttlecraft. He had finally reached the safety of the Space Cannon Zeus—that's all that mattered. It was good to feel zero gravity again, and to get away from the ground. Now he was ready to put the rest of his plan into effect.

At this point, he couldn't trust anyone but himself . . . to do what had to be done.

The dapper general straightened his uniform and moved briskly through the air lock, saluting soldiers as he went. He still had a sizable force at his command, but these soldiers and technicians weren't important. All that mattered was the weapon they controlled—the Zeus Cannon.

Holding his chin up, Hein headed into the control room and sat down at the communications display. On a holographic image, he could see the Executive Council down on Earth. They looked like frightened rabbits, or game pieces from a chess set. *My chess set.*

The chairman of the Council jumped to his feet and demanded, "What caused the Barrier to fail, General Hein?"

The general shrugged stiffly. "Ah, I am afraid it was only a matter of time before the Phantoms developed an immunity to our Barriers," he lied. "But I am relieved to see that you and the rest of the Council were able to evacuate to Houston without incident."

He waited, letting them squirm a little longer.

"It was a terrible loss suffered this evening," admitted the chairman. "The Council has reconsidered your proposal to fire the Zeus Cannon."

Hein kept his face immobile, trying not to show his joy and relief. At last, those monsters would feel the wrath of humanity. "I see," he answered.

"We are transmitting the access codes to you now," said the leader of the Council.

The computers whirred for a second as they recorded an incoming message. With satisfaction, the general watched the access codes scrawl across his screen. He had to fight the impulse to rub his hands together.

"And, General," said the chairman, "best of luck to us all."

Hein could stand no more of their simpering faces, and he turned off the holographic display. He wouldn't need luck—just enough firepower.

He rose to his feet and regarded the technicians gathered in the control room. "Prepare to fire the cannon," he ordered.

"The target, sir?" asked the worker on the tactical station.

With a smile, General Hein answered, "The Phantom crater."

CHAPTER 12

As the *Black Boa* descended from orbit, Aki took a good look at the Leonid Meteor, the source of all their problems. If Dr. Sid was right, it was also the source of the solution. But that almost seemed impossible, after all they had been through.

The meteor looked like a dull scab in the middle of a dark bruise. The land around the jagged crater was blackened and covered with wreckage and corpses. Phantoms were there, but invisible.

So many lives had been lost in futile attacks on that unearthly rock, including a nuclear attack, and now they were going to pay it a visit! As Gray said, would it be a one-way trip?

She couldn't worry about that now. Aki turned to look at Dr. Sid in the copilot seat, and he gave her a smile. "The Quatro is waiting, and so is Captain Edwards. I'll guide you to the eighth spirit."

"Keep the *Boa* close," she said. "But not too close."

Aki rose to her feet and walked briskly down the corridor. The sensation of gravity was odd after so many hours in weightlessness. Still it was good to return to Earth. While they were in orbit, it seemed as if they were hiding. Now they were going to face the enemy in their own lair.

She moved down the ladder into the cargo bay, where the small, four-wheeled ATV was waiting. Gray opened the door for her, and she stepped inside. He was all business as usual, but there was a warmth in his dark eyes.

"You ready?" he asked.

Aki touched her chest plate, which had been modified by Dr. Sid for this mission. She guessed that if they failed, there was no point in worrying about the infection in her body . . . or anything else, for that matter.

She nodded and flipped a switch. "Powering the shield."

Gray checked his holographic instruments. "Okay. We're over the meteor."

Thrusters blasting to slow its descent, the *Black Boa* hovered over the vast crater. Slowly the landing platform descended, with the Quatro hanging from it by cables.

Aki and Gray glanced worriedly at one another. More and more, this mission looked like certain death. But death was no stranger to either one of them. They forced themselves to study their read-outs and sensors, keeping their minds on business. Still, trying to find one Phantom out of millions was like looking for a match in a burning haystack.

Gray activated his radio. "Do you have it in sight, Doctor?"

"There are so many of them," answered Sid worriedly. After a moment, he broke in excitedly, "Wait! Yes. I'm tracking the eighth spirit moving along the crater's surface!"

Aki picked up the blip on her own sensors and nodded at Gray. He looked worried, because the Phantoms were rising to meet them. The monsters glowed brilliantly as they struck the Quatro's shield and were repelled. With each attack, the lights inside the ATV flickered. They would be safe in here only as long as the fuel cells held out.

"Now let's take a closer look," said Gray, using the cable winch to lower them.

The crater loomed as huge as a volcano, and Aki held her breath. She felt so exposed, hanging over the crater in their little vehicle, that she almost ordered them to retreat. Then Sid's voice broke over the radio. "It's a match!" he cried. "It's a perfect match!"

Aki let out her breath and gave Gray a smile. Maybe everything would work out, after all.

* * *

"Ready to fire Zeus Cannon in three minutes," said the technician on the tactical console. The control room of the space station was packed with technicians and soldiers, and General Hein sat in the command chair.

The operations officer reported, "Ovo-pacs at maximum. Transferring plasma flow to auto."

"Counterthrusters are engaged," said the pilot on navigation.

"Lox flow decoupled . . . status is green," said another engineer.

General Hein swiveled in his chair, smiling. It was time to blow all those fiendish Phantoms to pieces . . . to get revenge for his wife and daughter.

Suddenly an alarm sounded, and the technicians scurried to find the cause. It was the tactical officer who reported, "We have something on radar over the impact site, sir."

Hein leaped from his chair and strode to the man's console, gazing over his shoulder. He could see the tiny radar blip—it was some kind of vehicle, hovering over the crater.

"It's *her,*" he hissed angrily. It had to be Aki Ross.

"Sir?" asked the confused technician.

"Just a traitor under the influence of the enemy," answered Hein with disdain. "Continue the countdown. We'll take them all out at the same time."

With a smug look of satisfaction, General Hein returned to his seat. He watched the displays blazing all around him as the countdown continued. Finally the tactical station reported, "Target locked! Ready to fire on your command."

With a feeling of power and vengeance coursing through his veins, the general pointed his finger. "Fire."

On the outside of the space station, which had the shape of a giant white cannon, the ovo-tubes glowed with charged power. Thrusters engaged, and valves opened as the full brunt of bio-etheric energy was focused on a single target. The massive cannon began to spin, and a moment later it disgorged its brilliant white beam.

*   *   *

On the Quatro, Aki grinned with delight. All her sensors were lining up perfectly, and their target was in sight. "We're closing on the Phantom. Contact in thirty seconds."

"It's a perfect match," said Dr. Sid over the intercom. "I'm sending you data."

"We've got enough data," answered Gray. "Let's just get that spirit and get out of here."

They lowered ever closer to the lip of the meteor, where the colorful Phantom was almost cooperating by remaining in one place. *It might even rise to meet us,* thought Aki excitedly. She ran a quick check on her chest plate and found that the new device was working perfectly. It was all perfect, until—

An alarm sounded, then a blazing white light engulfed them, blinding Aki. She covered her eyes and screamed as the Quatro was tossed on the end of its cable like a Yo-Yo. It was all they could do to stay in their seats in the turbulence.

"There's a huge energy surge!" shouted Sid, but his voice was drowned out by static.

The meteor seemed to explode with a blinding light that turned the crater into a mass of seething life. Countless Phantoms oozed from the jagged hole in the middle, and it looked like an anthill from a feverish nightmare. Phantoms overflowed from the crater like an eruption of lava, and thousands of them whirled in the air.

"What was that?" asked Aki with a gasp.

"It's the Zeus," said Gray through clenched teeth. "They're firing on the crater."

Sid's voice broke through the static. "Aki? Captain? Are you all right?"

"Stand by," said Gray, working his instruments.

Aki managed to get a new sensor reading. With a sinking feeling, she saw that the blip was gone. "Sid, the eighth spirit is not on our scanner. Do you have it?"

There came a long silence before the doctor croaked, "The eighth spirit . . . has been destroyed."

It was like a knife had been plunged into her stomach, but Aki managed to say, "What are we going to do now?"

"Nothing," said Gray glumly. "This mission is over. We have to get outta here." They heard metal groaning from stress, and the captain looked up worriedly. "The cables—"

"Incoming!" shouted Sid, his voice booming in the Quatro.

Aki leaned over to look down at the crater. A second beam from the cannon beam bathed the meteor in white light, and something began to move in the depths of the rock. It looked like a Phantom, only it was gigantic—miles across—and it had millions of writhing tentacles. It was like the mother of all Phantoms . . . the mother of all nightmares!

"What is *that*?" whispered Gray in horror.

The young woman had no answer. All she could do was gasp as the twisting, churning monster rose from the crater, dwarfing it. Worse yet, the behemoth seemed to be headed straight toward them, its tentacles grasping for their tiny vehicle.

Aki gulped. "If you're gonna get us out of here, you better do it now!"

Before the captain could do anything, they heard the awful sound of metal wrenching . . . followed by a loud crack. The weakened cables snapped like rubber bands, and the tiny ATV plummeted through the air.

"Hold on!" shouted Gray as they dropped straight toward the writhing tentacles of the monster.

CHAPTER 13

As the Quatro dropped through the sky, Aki saw Gray pull a lever and shoot off the gel packs. The missiles exploded on the surface of the meteor, spreading a layer of foam that cushioned their fall. Still it was a hard jolt when the small ATV finally came to rest on the jagged rock.

Aki shook her head, trying to clear it. When she looked around, she was almost sorry she had. Phantoms swarmed around them—they bubbled from the center of the meteor like a backed-up sewer. Luckily, the shield still worked, and none of the ghastly creatures could enter their vehicle.

Gray sighed deeply beside her and rubbed his eyes. She knew how he felt—it was unbelievable that they were still alive. Their next unbelievable trick would be to get out of here.

Sid's voice broke through the crackle of static. "Come in . . . come in, please! Aki, Gray, can you hear me?"

"Yes," she answered. "Sid, I need to talk to the station. Can you patch us through?"

It took a few seconds, but finally the startled voice of a technician came over the radio. "Who's down there on the meteor?"

"Who's in charge?" she demanded. There wasn't time to waste talking to an underling.

"General Hein," came the answer. "He's listening."

Aki spelled it out for all of them. "General Hein, you must cease fire immediately. What you are looking at in the crater is the living spirit of an alien's home world."

All she got was a grunt for an answer, and she went on, "Their planet was destroyed, and part of it landed here. This is not an invasion. It never was."

"Oh, I see," said Hein sarcastically. "And what have we been fighting all this time, Doctor? *Ghosts?*"

"Yes," she answered. "Spirits that are confused, lost, and angry."

"Yeah, right. And these spirits are coming out of this 'Gaia' thing?"

"General Hein, you have to listen," she begged.

She heard him laugh. "Alien Gaia, Earth Gaia . . . Doctor, even if I believed in such nonsense, the fact remains the Earth is under attack from an aggressor who must be destroyed at all costs."

"The cost may be the entire planet, sir. Firing on the alien Gaia will only make it stronger." She balled her fists together, hoping he would listen.

"Well, since you are under the alien's influence, Doctor, I will take your protest to mean that we are in fact pursuing the correct course of action. So, I suggest you take your last few moments and prepare to meet your 'Gaia.' "

She heard him tell his men, "Continue to fire until the invader has been destroyed!"

The deadly beam continued to rain down upon them, and the Quatro was tossed back and forth like a toy. The earth itself began to crack around the crater, and huge fissures formed. Many of the Phantoms vaporized, but more and more poured forth to take their places.

The Phantom Gaia grew stronger from the bombardment of energy, and it towered above them like a skyscraper with tentacles. Gray gunned the engine of the Quatro, trying to drive away, but they were mired in cracks and dirt.

The Gaia suddenly whipped a huge tentacle straight toward them, and the tiny car was engulfed by the appendage. Sparks blasted off the shield, but the gigantic creature kept flailing around them, like an octopus.

A huge fissure opened beneath the ATV, and Aki gripped Gray's arm as the car turned on its side. She watched in horror as both they and the Gaia fell into the crack, plunging deeper into the center of the meteor.

* * *

Above them in the *Black Boa,* Dr. Sid had seen enough. He gripped the controls of the shuttlecraft and tried to get away from the Zeus Cannon.

The small craft spiraled to the surface, and the doctor managed to regain control just in time. With a hard jolt, he landed the *Black Boa* on the ground. But that was hardly safe either, because the Zeus Cannon was causing the ground to shift and break apart. It was like being in the middle of an earthquake.

Sid couldn't do anything but grip the arms of his chair and hang on tightly.

* * *

In orbit around the Earth, General Hein frowned at the latest readouts. Despite their constant bombardment, the Phantoms were not dying. In fact, they were spawning at an enormous rate. He couldn't see the big one right now, and he was still trying to figure out what it was. Along with that annoying Dr. Ross, this was not working as planned.

As usual, Dr. Sid's bio-etheric energy left something to be desired, Hein thought angrily. *What we need is more power.*

"General!" called the technician on the operations console. "The system is overheating, sir."

Hein banged his fist on his chair. "We're going to hit it again and again, and keep on hitting it. Until it's dead!"

"But sir, we're not even sure if it's having any effect on the creature!"

"No effect?" snapped Hein. "We've got them on the run, soldier. This is our moment of victory. I order you to fire."

The technician frowned at his readings. "The system won't allow us to fire again—"

"We'll see about that." The general jumped to his feet and strode out the door. *If these simpering fools won't do it, I'll turn off the safety overrides myself.*

*   *   *

Aki shook her head and could feel a large bump behind her ear. Somehow the Quatro had survived the second fall. *But where are we?* Gray blinked at her, glad to see that she was all right. Then he turned his attention to the instrument panel, which was beeping a warning.

After a moment, Gray muttered, "Our shield is out. We're sitting ducks in here. Come on."

With considerable effort, the big man managed to pry open his door. He grabbed a weapon and climbed out, then helped Aki to crawl out. She saw that the Quatro had survived because gel packs cushioned the landing. But they were still trapped on a ledge in the middle of a huge gash in the Earth.

On an upper ledge was the enormous Phantom, the alien Gaia. It looked like some kind of giant heart—a pulsing mass of blood and veins spreading outward into the soil. Aki glanced down and saw that the gorge went much deeper—to other ledges.

"This is not a good place to be," said Gray with a

scowl. Holding Aki's arm, he stepped forward and looked over the edge of the ridge. Aki did likewise, and she gasped when she saw what was beneath them.

It looked like an ocean—a shimmering mass of blue. Only it wasn't water; it was like a Phantom, but solid and beautiful. As the enormous mass of blue undulated beneath them, Aki felt a warmth within her chest, and a tear of joy eased from her eye.

"What is that?" asked Gray warily. "That's not what I think it is, is it?"

"Yes," she answered. "It's Gaia. The spirit of our Earth."

Gray looked worriedly at the Phantom Gaia writhing above them—red and angry—then at the blue Gaia floating serenely below them. He gulped. "This is *definitely* not a good place to be."

Aki was so deep in thought that she didn't reply, and he shook her arm. "Hey, are you all right?"

"I'm fine," she answered calmly. "I have to talk to Dr. Sid. I hope our comm signal still works."

Aki moved to the Quatro and grabbed the headset, activating the comm link. "Sid? Do you read me?"

"Go ahead," came a familiar voice. "I crash-landed, but I'm still here. I think I dislocated my shoulder."

"We're looking at Gaia!" she said excitedly. "Do you hear me, Sid? Earth's Gaia! I think this explains why the eighth spirit appeared here." She held her breath until she got a response.

"Yes, yes! That's it!" he exclaimed. "That explains my readings! Newer particles merging with the older ones—a kind of reincarnation."

His words tumbled out, "A single Phantom must have come into contact with a new spirit born from our own Gaia. If so, it would have been given a different energy signature that set it apart from the other Phantoms."

Gray looked curiously at Aki, and she gave him a smile. Sid's voice broke in, "Oh, you two could not have hoped for a better location to find a new compatible spirit. Whatever you do, don't move! Stay right where you are!"

"Staying right where we are may not be as easy as it sounds," said Gray. He lifted his weapon and fired at an ugly Phantom that was drifting toward them. The thing vaporized in the deadly beam.

"Don't shoot any of them!" yelled Sid urgently. "You could very well destroy our last hope."

"Then what do you suggest I do, Doctor?" asked Gray. "Ask them to play nice?"

"Combat strategy is your area of expertise, Captain, not mine."

While they argued, Aki slipped into the Quatro and checked the readings on the holograph. After a moment, she saw the familiar blip. The eighth spirit—it had returned!

"Sid!" called Aki, "I have a reading here in the fissure. Do you see it?"

"Yes!" answered the doctor. "A compatible spirit. Maybe Earth's Gaia is creating new spirits. It must be very near you."

Gray looked worriedly upward, where a dozen Phantoms were floating down. He aimed his gun to fire, but hesitated. "Well, which one is it? *Which one?*"

As Phantoms began to threaten them, Gray climbed a pile of rubble to a higher ledge. He was trying to draw them away from the Quatro and Aki. If he couldn't fire at the Phantoms, there wasn't much else he could do but divert them.

Sid's worried voice came over the radio. "I'm . . . I'm having difficulty narrowing it down. Just a moment, please."

Gray scowled as if he couldn't believe the mess they were in. He dodged the Phantoms as best he could, but there wasn't much room to maneuver on the narrow ledge. They would be overwhelmed in seconds!

"Doctor, it's getting crowded in here!" he shouted.

As the Phantoms swirled all around him, Gray looked back to the Quatro. "Aki, we don't have much time. Aki!" He stared into the vehicle and saw her slumped in her seat, unconscious. "Aki!"

A Phantom lashed out at him, and Gray was forced to fire. No matter how many he killed, they kept coming. . . .

CHAPTER 14

Once again, Aki stood on the alien wasteland she had visited so often in her dreams. The bodies of countless Phantom soldiers littered the landscape, as far as she could see. There was a tug on her chest, and she looked down to see the alien particles within her, swirling with agitation.

Suddenly the alien particles leaped from her chest and burrowed into the ground, where an alien soldier had fallen. At once, his armor fell away and was absorbed into the red sand, just as a blue spirit circled upward. These new spirits created a living Phantom soldier, who towered above her.

This stoic soldier pointed toward the ragged landscape. Everywhere, the spirits of the aliens were standing over their own bodies, which slowly sank into the ground. Aki gasped as vegetation began to grow all over the barren field. She stepped back, not wanting to squash these new sprigs of life, but plants pushed through the soil. The alien planet was coming back to life!

* * *

Aki awoke with a start and found herself inside the damaged Quatro midway down the fissure. There was movement on the ledge above her, and she could see Gray, dodging the Phantoms. Aki activated the device on her chest, and she wasn't surprised to see that the Phantom particles within her had disappeared. She was cured of the infestation!

Not only that, but the holograph showed a new spirit wave, glowing bright and strong.

"I have it!" she shouted. "The eighth spirit!"

Gray turned and gaped at her, and she motioned to him. "Gray, get in here. I need you!"

She quickly contacted Sid on the *Black Boa* and told him the marvelous news. "Have you been listening, Doctor? The wave pattern is complete!"

"Yes, I read you!" he shouted excitedly. "Th-this is wonderful! But I . . . I don't see how you could have found the final spirit—"

"It found me, Doctor." Aki used a patch cable to

connect her chest device to the communications panel on the Quatro. As she transmitted her findings, she watched Gray still fighting the Phantoms. They almost seemed to welcome the deadly beams that sent them home.

Sid's voice broke in. "Oh, my word! I see now. I understand!"

After shooting a final blast, Gray jumped into the Quatro and stared at her. "Well, I don't understand! What's going on?"

Aki ignored his question as she pulled out the damaged fuel cells. "Give me your ovo-pac. I need to power up the shield!"

The captain frowned as he took the power supply from his weapon. "But we'll be defenseless—"

"Just do it!"

With a grunt, he tossed her the fuel pack, and she used it to replace the spent pack under the dashboard. Gray looked worriedly out the window as the Phantoms massed for another attack. "I hope you know what you're doing, Aki."

"We have to project the completed wave back to Sid," she explained.

"What?"

"Sid's theory was right. I have it—the eighth spirit. I'm cured, Gray." She continued to work on the wiring.

He shook his head doubtfully. "Are you sure you have the final spirit?"

"Yes, yes, I'm sure," she answered impatiently.

"But how? H-how can you know that?"

She smiled. "Don't worry. A Phantom told me."

Gray scowled. "Oh . . . great." Suddenly he shouted in alarm as a Phantom tentacle penetrated the tiny vehicle.

Aki hit a switch and said, "That's it. Shield on!"

But nothing happened. The tentacle kept probing for life, and Gray had to duck to avoid it. He reached for his weapon, then realized that it had no power.

"It's not working!" he shouted. "We have to do something before it's too late!" He tried to grab back the ovo-pac he had given her.

Aki placed her hand over his, and her calm eyes locked onto his frightened eyes. "If this doesn't work, then it's already too late. Gray, trust me."

With a nod, he released the ovo-pac. They held hands as the Phantom tentacles converged around them. At the last moment, the shield blinked on, and the tentacles vanished in a flash of light. Outside the window, the eerie shapes glistened as they struck the shield. Aki noted that the color of the shield was now a deep blue . . . as blue as the Earth's Gaia.

The scientist and the captain held each other. Their fears and anxieties seemed to melt in the tender embrace. When Aki pulled away, she hit the switch and released the energy wave stored in the chest plate.

At once, the beams of energy began radiating upward from the Quatro, bathing the Phantom Gaia hovering overhead. As the shimmering energy waves engulfed the Gaia, it began to change colors—from angry red to soothing blue. Aki gazed at Gray and smiled with deep satisfaction.

* * *

On the Zeus Station high in orbit over the Earth, General Hein also smiled with satisfaction. He had overridden the safety mechanisms, and now there was nothing to prevent him from firing the Zeus Cannon as much as he wanted.

"I'll blast you all to bits!" vowed the general, shaking his fist at the target in his sights. With a grin, he pushed the firing button.

* * *

On the Quatro, Aki studied her instruments and frowned. Only one thing could be causing this much adverse radiation, and she looked upward.

The blazing beam of the Zeus Cannon engulfed them a second later.

"Oh, no! *No!*" she shouted angrily.

Gray threw her to the floor of the vehicle and covered her with his own body. The Quatro began to shake and fall apart like a shack in a hurricane. The sky seemed to darken as the Phantom Gaia on the ledge above again turned a fiery red.

*   *   *

"Warning! System overload!" said the computer in the Zeus control room.

"I know," muttered Hein, still punching the firing button.

"Warning! System overload!"

"I *knowww!*" howled the general. "But it must be done."

Suddenly it became unbearably hot inside the space station. Hein could hear technicians banging on the door, trying to get in. *The fools are panicking as usual,* thought the general. *Am I the only one with any guts?*

Hein could see every gauge on his console go into the red zone. Through the viewport, the immense ovo-pacs on the side of the station glowed with white heat. An explosion sounded somewhere in the orbital station—probably the Habitat Area. He heard screams outside the door, and the beam from the cannon weakened.

The general banged the firing button. "Fire! Fire right now! Come on, do it for me. . . . Fire! Argh, stupid system—"

Outside the viewport, he saw a chunk of the space station floating toward him. "Uh-oh—"

The Habitat Area smashed into the control room; an explosion shook him out of his seat. With a scream, General Hein was sucked into space. The last thing he saw was the entire Zeus Station turn into a roaring fireball. Like a metal meteor, it plunged into the Earth's atmosphere.

*   *   *

From the cockpit of the *Black Boa,* Sid watched in horror as the alien Gaia grew and grew under the white beam. Its tentacles writhed with agony, and it looked like a giant red sun going nova. Phantoms again erupted from cracks in the meteor, and they flew across the landscape in every direction.

This time, it really did look like the end of the world. Then, without warning, the terrible beam stopped blasting the crater. Sid looked up and saw the clouds clearing above the blackened desert.

Was this the end, or the beginning?

* * *

As the Zeus Cannon scorched the crater, rocks plummeted down, turning the Quatro into a hunk of twisted metal. Aki slumped down in her chair, waiting for the bombardment to end. Mercifully, it finally did. She heard groans, and she turned to see Gray beside her. He was gripping his stomach and bleeding from his head. He looked badly injured.

In desperation, she opened the door and managed to drag him out. He was conscious, but barely, and she laid him in the red dust. Their only hope was to contact the *Black Boa* and get help from Sid, although she feared the shuttlecraft was in bad shape, too.

"Sid, come in!" she shouted into the wireless. She called over and over again, but there was no answer.

Finally she returned to the captain and propped him against a rock. "Gray! Don't leave me, Gray."

He took a raspy breath. "I told Sid this was a one-way trip. Looks like I was right."

"No, Gray, hang on, please," she said, fighting back tears. "I need you!"

"Aki—" he breathed, clutching her hand, "we are going to make it. Help me stand up."

Fighting back her emotions, Aki pulled the captain to his feet. He staggered for a bit and gripped his stomach, but he managed to stay upright. From the trickle of blood on his mouth, she realized he must have more serious internal injuries.

Aki gripped his arm, filled with fear. She could tell from his lifeless eyes that Gray was dying.

"Listen to me," he said with difficulty. "You saved my life once. Now I want you to save yourself." He pulled away from her and began to climb to a higher ledge, closer to the pulsing alien Gaia.

"Gray, no! Please!" she cried.

"Let me do this, Aki," he rasped. "Trust me."

"Don't leave me, Gray!"

The captain paused for a moment. "You've been trying to tell me that death isn't the end. Don't back out on me . . . now that I finally believe."

Higher he climbed over the rubble, as if trying to reach the Phantom Gaia.

"I need you, Gray!" she cried.

But he was too high above her to respond. With effort, he straightened his back, as if coming to attention. Then he lifted his arms and reached toward the Phantom Gaia, releasing his own shimmering blue spirit wave.

At once, the eighth spirit within Aki shot from her body and connected to Gray. Finally complete, the combined spirit wave flowed upward into the heart of the Phantom Gaia.

"I love you," said Gray, his voice booming in her ears and her heart. Aki saw his lifeless body fall, and she tried to hang on to his shining spirit for as long as she could. Although Gray was gone, his spirit blossomed upward and outward, changing everything as it flowed across the wasteland.

The Phantom Gaia turned cloudy and white, until it gradually faded away. Aki felt a great joy along with her grief. The Gaia of that alien planet, marooned on Earth along with millions of spirits, was finally going home. The spiritual and the physical would be reunited on that distant planet.

* * *

Inside the *Black Boa,* Sid watched the renewal of the Earth with a smile on his face. As the spirits rushed by him in the form of playful balls, the old scientist was suffused with warmth.

Sid felt as if Aki were beside him, and Captain Gray, too. He knew the captain was dead, because it was his spirit that had bonded all the others. But

Aki was alive! According to his instruments, she was just below him—on a ledge in the crevasse.

Working his holographic instruments, the doctor quickly lowered the landing platform down to her. *If only all the Deep Eyes could be here,* he thought, *that would be fitting.*

But they must know their sacrifice was not in vain. They bought the people of Earth precious time—enough time to understand the true nature of the Phantoms.

* * *

As Aki rode on the platform to the top of the crater, she could see the Earth blossoming like a day in spring. A brilliant sunrise bathed the land, giving every pebble a golden glow. Despite her grief, the young woman felt enormous pride in what they had done. She knew the Earth had been reborn, along with the alien planet so far away.

The young woman heard a cry, and she looked up to see the hawk, flying joyously overhead.

About the Author

JOHN VORNHOLT has had several writing and performing careers, ranging from being a stuntman to writing animated cartoons, but he enjoys writing books most of all. He likes playing one-on-one with the reader. John has written almost twenty *Star Trek* novels, plus novels set in such diverse universes as *Sabrina, the Teenage Witch* and *Dinotopia*. His fantasy novel about Aesop, *The Fabulist,* is being adapted as a musical for the stage, and he has a new fantasy novel, *The Troll King,* coming out next year.

John lives in Arizona with his wife, Nancy, and two kids, Sarah and Eric, and he likes to go roller skating and snow skiing. Please visit his web page at: www.sff.net/people/vornholt.